SILVER MOON

GREAT NOVELS
OF
EROTIC DOMINATION
AND
SUBMISSION

NEW TITLES EVERY MONTH

www.smbooks.co.uk

TO FIND OUT MORE ABOUT OUR READERS' CLUB WRITE
TO;

SILVER MOON READER SERVICES;
Barrington Hall Publishing
Hexgreave Hall
Farnsfield
Nottinghamshire NG22 8LS
Tel; 01157 141616

YOU WILL RECEIVE A FREE MAGAZINE OF EXTRACTS
FROM OUR EXTENSIVE RANGE OF EROTIC FICTION
ABSOLUTELY FREE. YOU WILL ALSO HAVE THE
CHANCE TO PURCHASE BOOKS WHICH ARE
EXCLUSIVE TO OUR READERS' CLUB

***

NEW AUTHORS ARE WELCOME

Please send submissions to;
Barrington Hall Publishing
Hexgreave Hall
Farnsfield N22 8LS

Silver Moon books are an imprint of Barrington Hall Publishing
which is part of Barrington Hall Ltd.

ISBN 978-1-907475-06-1

All characters and events depicted are entirely fictitious; any resemblance to anyone living or dead is entirely coincidental

HEART IN A BOX
(TRUE CONFESSIONS 4)

by

Syra Bond

PREFACE

Sometimes, it feels as though I have spent my whole life in captivity, or slavery, or under the control of another in some way. And there has been so much pain, and suffering, and fear. I shiver when I think of it. I have been taken to the limits in so many ways – so many different punishments, so much hurt – but, even as I have screamed and yelled that I could take no more, I have been filled with the urgency of my own pleasure. The pain itself brings something with it that is uncontrollable – its own delight, yes, but also the promise of joy so ultimate that beyond it there is nothing. It is this terrible need that stalks me. When I am being whipped or spanked, when my flesh is stinging from mistreatment, or I am gasping with the terror of being overfilled, or quenching my thirst with semen. When I am subjected to any of these things within me there is always a growing scent of pleasure. Yes, it's like something I can smell – a perfume, an aroma that eventually overtakes me, sucks up my suffering, converts it into something beyond pain, and brings me to extremes of ecstasy that leave me gasping for breath in another world. Yes, it is exactly like that, it is as if I transcend all of this world and am transported to another. I am addicted to it and the means by which I can find it – addicted to this beautiful suffering because it is only when I suffer that my transcendence can be complete. Yes, suffering is my pathway to guaranteed pleasure. No matter how much I have suffered it has always led me to the heavenly delights. This has been both my downfall and my only desire; my descent into the horrors of suffering has always been accompanied by my ascent to rapture.

When finally I escaped from Father Dawson – the harshest and cruellest of my captors – I thought my life would change, that at last I could free myself of the need for pain. I thought that I could find pleasure like others, from simple satisfaction, contact, and excitement. But I was mistaken. Even from the dead he brought me almost unbearable torture and with it came again the excrucation of overwhelming joy. And this time there was another, more terrible legacy. His own evil spawned something worse even that his joy of the infliction of pain and suffering. He found that within me was the germ of a terrible bloodlust. I was unaffected by the infection within me but ingestion of my blood brought a horrifying change in others – each lost their human life in exchange for the dark consuming life of a vampire. My blood condemned them to an existence focused only on lusting for blood and flesh. And from me they also took my appetite for joy through pain. Their life, a combination of the pleasures of pain and joy with the insatiable need for the drinking of hot blood was what they owed to me.

The legacy of Father Dawson's cruelty in his followers brought me into their fold – I too became infected with my own germ, but the sacrifice of another led me to be saved. But it was not a complete cure. I still carry the germ. I have delighted in the pleasures of blood myself and it will not leave me – the draw of it is too strong. Even though an antidote now runs in my veins, it is accompanied by a latent desire for the taste of blood of which I cannot rid myself. I can control it sometimes, but it is a battle. Whenever pain overtakes me, and my ecstasy erupts, so does the desire to sink my teeth into the flesh of another, the need to taste the hot ambrosia that runs within them, to drink it, to refresh myself with it, to nourish myself with it. No, I am not cured – the infection is only kept at bay, and barely at that.

And those that have been infected by my spore pursue me. They are a flock, a rabble of lost souls in need of a focus. In the absence of Father Dawson, they want to be close to their progenitor – and that is me. Their need is no respecter of my wishes. I do not know if I can escape them, but for my own safety I must try. Nor do I know if I can suppress my own needs – but for my own sanity that too I must try.

Syra Bond
Bratisalava
2009

1. ESCAPE!

They didn't believe my story to start with. The fact that I was there standing in the office of the Bayview District Police Station convinced them I wasn't dead, and that was a start, but that I was actually me – that was a different matter. They'd actually got my passport there – God knows how – but they didn't plan on handing it over just like that. They had lots of forms – and they all had to be filled in correctly! This was San Francisco, U.S.A. – not a place for inexactitude!

It was already dark. The fluorescent lights inside the station were dim but harsh. Multicoloured window blinds at all the windows were pulled down.

'This is the S.F.P.D ma'am,' said the sergeant. 'And we've got regulations.' He hitched up his black leather belt and held the grip of the heavy black revolver that was squeezed tightly into the shiny holster at his hip. 'Where would we be without them? That's right isn't it officers?' He nodded to two young police officers seated behind him in front of computer screens. They nodded back enthusiastically. One was a beautiful young woman in shorts with long hair. A shimmering weight of velvet black curls hung about her pale, smooth skinned, and wide mouthed face. As she turned and removed her sunglasses, her luscious mane moved in a slow wave. It shone in the harsh fluorescent light – abundant, glorious, mesmerising – like the Pacific swell on a warm starlit night, catching the phosphorescent light beneath the skin thin surface in magical glistening sparks. The man smiled thinly. He looked ashen. He pushed his hand down the front of his trousers, hitched up his weighty cock and smiled again.

Three hours later I was still there, standing at the high, bar-like desk trying to fit the right answers into the appropriate boxes. Every time I made a mistake they made me start again with a fresh form.

The beautiful woman smiled at me. Her white teeth shone. The sight of them thrilled me. She turned back to her work and threw her mass of hair back onto her shoulders. There was no insignia of rank on her blue shirt; its buttons strained against her tightly pulled breasts. She looked so young and inexperienced. I leant forward and read the motto on her shoulder patch: "*Oro en paz, fierro en guerra*" – "*Gold in peace, iron in war*". She smiled again and this time her smooth pale cheeks flushed with embarrassment. Her teeth were truly beautiful – even, large, the canines slightly proud of the general line both top and bottom, and all perfectly white.

My head was aching – it was hot and one of the fluorescent lights was flickering. I took a conical paper cup and filled it from the iced water machine. I was thirsty and tipped it too fast against my lips. It sloshed out, dribbled down my chin and dripped all down the front of my thin white shirt. I looked down. I could see right through it! My nipples were hard and poking up against the translucent material. I felt them aching – deep and penetrating. The wet material clung to them and drew out a profound painful yearning from within my breasts. I wanted to touch them, squeeze them, pinch them. I coughed and held my hand to my mouth just so that I could rub my forearm across them. They tingled at the contact and I breathed in deeply to try and ease it. But I didn't want to ease it. I did it again but only quickly and the briefness of my touch only increased my frustration. The aching went even deeper – right down into my hips.

I could feel the male police officer's leering eyes on me as I walked back to the desk. I know my cheeks were red. I asked for a fresh pen and carried on working with the forms. As I wrote my answer to the heading

"Next of Kin" I couldn't stop myself imagining going again to the drinks machine and spilling some more water, this time on purpose, over each of my breasts. I could almost feel the cool water wetting my shirt and sucking my nipples against it. I squeezed the tops of my thighs together as the yearning ache went again into my hips. I felt my cheeks reddening again as I pictured my embarrassment, this time not only because I could not disguise my hard nipples pressing through the wet material, but because I had done it on purpose. Surely they would be able to guess!

About an hour later – and after starting another form because I got mixed up over how long I had been in the US – a tall man wearing heavy sunglasses and a dark suit walked lazily through the double doors. He had a muscular build and his face was tanned.

'FBI,' he said flashing a card and pushing it back quickly into the inside pocket of his jacket. 'You have a Syra Bond here. I need to talk to her.'

Hearing my name like that was a shock. A wave of nervousness spread into my stomach; it was as if I had done something wrong and should feel guilty.

The sergeant looked up from behind the desk. He nodded towards me.

'Yes sir, we sure do. That's her. Still having trouble with our forms, I think. But, as I say, where would we be without them? You can use our interview room.'

It was a tiny room, just two hard backed chairs, a small square table between them set beneath another flickering fluorescent tube that hung on rusty chains above it.

With a wave of his hand the man told me to sit down. I was glad to get off my feet.

He stared at my prominent nipples, pressing hard against the still wet material of my shirt – two dark pink circles with a delectable hard centre. I drew my thighs together and felt their pressure on the soft flesh of my cunt. I felt flustered under his penetrating gaze. I checked the buttons on my shirt – just to distract myself and escape his hard stare. My face reddened with embarrassment and I licked my dry lips. I felt guilty in his presence – it was as if I was awaiting punishment for a crime I did not know I had committed.

'I think you know why I'm here, Syra.'

'No ... no, I don't,' I said nervously, still looking down and fiddling with the buttons of my shirt. 'Unless ... unless it's about Father Dawson? Is it about him? Is it about Father Dawson?'

'Father Dawson is dead, Syra. You know that, of course. But he wanted you to stay at Pacific Heights. It was his wish. Pacific Heights is your rightful place. He would have been very troubled to know you had left. Syra, you need to go back.'

I couldn't believe what he was saying. I had only just got away! I had been locked up there for I don't know how long – tortured, treated as a captive, bitten by insane people lusting for blood! He couldn't really be suggesting I should go back!

I went into a fidgeting panic. I wanted to run.

'No, no, I couldn't. I just couldn't! It's ridiculous! You can't imagine what I suffered there. No, no, I couldn't go back. It's impossible!'

My hands were shaking.

He removed his sunglasses, smiled condescendingly and sat on the table. He spread his legs wide, reached over and laid his hand on my shoulder. There was a thick pallid band of skin around his neck – even paler than his face – as though he had been wearing a tight collar since birth. As he turned – halfway between his ear and the whitish ring that encircled his throat – I saw two red blotched punctures in the skin of his neck. I went cold and pulled back but he grabbed the collar of my shirt and held me fast. The material yanked up against my nipples. The yearning ache came again between my hips. I drew in breath sharply.

My panic made me angry.

'How do you know I'm from Pacific Heights anyway?' I said struggling to get away from his grip. 'What's this all about? How did you find me here?'

I tried to pull his hand away but he tightened his hold on my shirt and twisted it up in his clenched fingers.

I choked and coughed.

'Syra, you must return. It is your rightful place, to be amongst the flock. They are part of you and you must be with them. They owe their new life to you. They need you. They depend on you.'

I felt suddenly stupid! I realised what was happening! He was one of them! He was one of Father Dawson's flock! Of course! He was one of the blood suckers from Pacific Heights and he had been sent to bring me back! The thought of it made me dizzy. My heart was thumping madly in my chest. The veins in my neck were throbbing. Suddenly, I thought of my blood being forced through my arteries under pressure, the idea of it returning from all parts of my body, along my veins, to my lungs, filled me with a surge of excitement. I couldn't suppress it. I felt giddy with confusion.

'You're one of them! You've come to take me back!' I screeched still struggling to break his grip. 'You're one of them!'

He grinned. His pointed canine teeth glinted in the harsh fluorescent light. He rubbed the puncture marks in his neck. It was as if massaging them gave him pleasure, as if either the feeling of pressure against them, or just the touch of his caressing fingers opened up again the pleasurable memory of when he had received them. I imagined opening up the wounds afresh, pressing my hollow canine teeth into the rounded holes, sucking, finding the strongest flow, slurping at the nectar, feeding on it. I couldn't keep my thoughts back. My mind was in turmoil.

I still wanted to run though. I knew that. Even as images of blood filled my mind, I still knew that. Yes, at least that made sense. Whatever my other desires were, they were still overpowered by my need to escape.

Pulling against his grip on my shirt, I turned to the door. I wondered if I could run to it and get away. My heart was pounding louder and louder – its thumping filled my giddy head. I could not compel myself to move. He gripped my shirt tighter. I choked again. It pulled harder against my nipples. Angrily, he snatched at it. It twisted around my left nipple, pinched it tightly and pulled it painfully. I shrieked.

The door opened. The sergeant and the two other police officers came in. I expected them to rush over and drag me from this man's clutches but instead they just wandered over nonchalantly.

'Not having trouble, I hope? There are a couple of problems with these forms.'

They completely ignored the fact that I was screaming and struggling against this man who had my shirt wound up viciously around my neck.

The sergeant held out the papers. The 'FBI' man scowled and dragged me angrily to my feet.

'I don't think we need worry too much about the forms, sergeant. This interview is at an end. She's coming with me.'

He yanked at my arm, pinched his fingers into my skin and dug them deep.

I looked at the beautiful woman in shorts. She tossed her mane of hair back and smiled. Her teeth captivated me. I pulled myself towards her.

'Please, can you help me? Please, he's not who he says he is.'

'She's a fugitive,' said my captor pushing past the beautiful woman. 'They've always got a tale. I'm pleased you managed to find her; and new to the job too by the looks of it. I am very grateful, sergeant. Good work.'

'Always willing to help,' said the sergeant. I tried to break free. The sergeant jumped back. 'She really is a minx!'

I struggled against the 'FBI' man's grip as he dragged me towards the door. I stumbled but he held my full weight by the shirt and pulled me along bodily. I choked and thought I was going to vomit.

'Here, let us help.' The sergeant stepped forward. 'Least we can do.'

He told the two officers to grab my legs. They lifted me off the ground. I struggled and fought against them. I twisted and threw myself from side to side. I couldn't believe what was happening. It was terrifying.

'On here! Put her on here!'

They carried me to the table and pushed me down backwards onto it.

I thrashed my legs and caught the backs of my calves on the edge of the table. I shouted out in pain.

The female officer pressed herself down onto me to try and hold me fast. Her long black hair fell across my face. It smelled sweet and clean. It lay across my skin like a silk cloth. I inhaled it deeply. She pressed down harder. I felt her breasts against mine. I knew she could feel mine too. I saw her neck. I reached my mouth up towards it. I placed my lips against her skin. It was smooth and firm. I could not resist the urge. I opened my mouth and ran the edges of my teeth against her skin. The contact thrilled me. It ran through my whole body in a massive wave. I lifted myself involuntarily.

I felt her pressing down harder on me to hold me in place. The confinement, the inability to move, the lack of physical freedom, all conspired to excite me with another wave of joy.

I opened my mouth wider. I increased the pressure against her skin. I felt the throbbing artery – I saw it in my mind, pulsating with crimson blood, fresh from her heart, filled with oxygen, with life itself.

They held me down firmly. The beautiful woman pulled herself back; her hair swished across my face like a gentle whip. It caught the tip of my tongue and stung it. I pulled it into my mouth. The next thing I knew I had been turned over and thrown onto my front.

I gasped for air as I felt the weight of the beautiful woman against my back. It must have been her companion who was holding my legs – I couldn't move them at all. The sergeant was strutting around me dangling his shiny chromium handcuffs in his hands. He bent down, rattled them in my face and grinned

Suddenly, I felt tension in my arms as they were yanked up behind me. I gasped for breath. I felt the narrow cold steel bands of the handcuffs around my wrists. They were pulled up quickly on their serrated ends and snapped shut. Each one was given an extra click of tension – an extra notch on their ratcheted clasps. They pinched my skin. I felt the blood pulsating in my hands.

They pulled me off the table and held me in a standing position. I was gasping, and too breathless to speak. The beautiful woman was on my left, holding onto my arm, the young male officer was on my right, his fingers digging deeply into the pressure point in my upper arm.

I slumped as my knees went weak. The two officers stopped me from falling. I felt giddy and wanted to vomit.

'Put her on her knees!' commanded the 'FBI' man. 'She needs to understand what is expected of her.'

They dropped me to my knees. I looked up at the 'FBI' man. He frowned.

'Syra, I thought you had learnt obedience under the instruction of Father Dawson. It is disappointing to find you have so quickly forgotten his orders. But I have not. He has passed the flock onto me. It is I, Pastor Wick, to whom you are answerable. I know you have been punished many times before. Obviously I need to remind you of the sting that pain can bring about, and the way of rightfulness that it can point to.' He stood back. 'Make her ready!'

The beautiful woman ripped open the front of my shirt and pulled it down. It hung like a rag on my arms. They pulled me back to the edge of the table and bent me forward across it. One of them pulled up my short skirt so that the hem was around my waist. My panties were yanked down in harsh jerks until they were just above my knees.

It must have been the sergeant who turned my head and pressed my face against the smooth top of the table. I was gasping loudly, still unable to speak, still petrified and filled with shock at the suddenness and ferocity of the attack. My arms were lifted higher so that they were completely clear of my now naked exposed bottom.

I squirmed but it was pointless – handcuffed, it was impossible to escape, and the weight of the officers' bodies as they pressed down on me meant I could hardly move. I knew my cunt was wet – I felt its flesh as I squirmed my hips and legs – and the thought of it being seen between my upturned buttocks sent a wave of embarrassment through me.

I waited – I don't know what for. I felt overcome with confusion, embarrassment and fear. I smelled the beautiful woman's hair – it was spread across my face.

I inhaled her breath. Her mouth was right by mine – I heard her breathing, swallowing, licking her lips! Terrified as I was, the sound of it still sent thrills through my body. Her licking lips struck up a rhythm with my pounding heart. I matched her breathing with mine.

Suddenly I jerked back, even against the tight handcuffs and the weight of the two officers pressing down on me I rose up and strained. I could not tell if it was a belt, or a strap or even a thick whip, but I knew it was leather, I knew it was smooth, I knew it had hard edges and I knew it was brought down with great force. I dropped back – forced back by the weight on top of me, relieved as the sting began to reduce. My heart was pounding even faster. I smelled the beautiful woman's warm breath – she was panting, as if she too had felt the pain of the cutting stroke across my buttocks.

Another smacking crack came down across my upturned bottom. There was no warning. I did not hear a swishing sound, nor the grunt of effort as the flail was wielded. I did not see the look in the eye of a punisher as he anticipated the delight of seeing the strap he wielded coming down, slapping down, against my tender taut skin. I yelped and rose up again, and again I was crushed back onto the hard surface of the table by the weight of my captors. I gasped, I shuddered, I wanted to scream but could not get enough breath.

I felt the heat of the beautiful woman's breath – I knew her mouth must be so close to mine, her white teeth so near, her soft wet tongue perhaps able to touch mine if she reached it out and probed it into my mouth. I stared ahead, looking for her without turning my head, expecting her to press her mouth against mine, to stifle my pain, to suck at my spit as she licked my tongue.

Another cracking blow came down. I was gripped with another seizure of pain, another spasm of involuntary effort as I rose and again, crushed by the weight of others, I fell against the table, and was filled with the pain of my punishment. My cunt ached; the strap had caught its soft edges. I tightened my buttocks then relaxed them. I opened them. For a moment I couldn't believe what I was doing! I waited for the next hoping this time that the strap would cut into the edges of my cunt again, but this time more deeply, more painfully, more deliberately.

I shrieked as it came down. I tightened the tops of my thighs around the pain but it was deep inside me – in my hips, my chest, my head. I could hardly bear it. I turned my head and my face was against the beautiful woman's mouth.

She opened her lips and licked out her tongue. She ran the sharp edges of her teeth along my chin and down the front of my throat. I felt her pulling them at the side of my neck. I felt the tightness as she closed them against my skin. I let my head drop to the side – opening myself to her, offering myself, wanting her to take my blood, wanting her to feed on me.

Another smacking blow came down. I shrieked again, I felt the increased pressure of her teeth on my neck. My desire rose in heavy waves. The pressure of the weight above me made me gasp for breath. I submitted completely. I listened for the rush of blood as she took it. I waited to be her food.

Suddenly, I was on the floor, twisting on my side.

The beautiful woman was being dragged off me by the 'FBI' man and the sergeant. They pulled her to her feet, tore open the front of her shirt and exposed her pink, tight fitting bra.

'You are out of control!' yelled the sergeant. 'How dare you try to feed like this? You know this is the carrier of the germ. You know she is to be treated properly. The punishment is to her taste. It is to satisfy her. It is not an excuse for you to take her valuable blood.'

'I'm so sorry, sir. Forgive me, please. I was overwhelmed, to be so close to her, the carrier – '

'That's enough whining. Officer! Handcuff her to the pegs on the wall. And remove her shorts and panties. She will feel some of the punishment for herself. We shall see if she takes it as well! We shall see if the germ has given her the same taste for the pleasure of pain that is locked within the carrier of the germ.'

The male officer pulled her up again the wall where a heavy coat peg was fixed. He felt his belt, looking for his handcuffs – he had left them in the office.

'Remove these!' shouted the sergeant angrily as he held up my wrists. 'Remove them!'

The officer unclipped the handcuffs from my wrists and secured the beautiful woman instead. Relieved of the tension around my wrists, and suddenly free of their bondage, I collapsed on the floor. I pulled my knees up to my chin and felt the soft edges of my cunt squeezed between the tops of my thighs.

The officer hung the beautiful woman onto the peg on the wall. She slumped against it as he pulled down her shorts to her ankles then ripped down her pink panties. She twisted slowly from side to side in fearful anticipation of the pain that was to come.

The 'FBI' man – Pastor Wick – pulled back a wide black belt and brought it down against her taut, rounded buttocks. There was loud crack as the leather made contact with her skin, then a penetrating shriek of pain as she felt its anger. She twisted the full weight of her body heavily on the peg, stretching the well defined muscles in her arms and thighs. Another blow came down and she shrieked again. She turned her head. Her mass of hair was tangled and wet across her tear soaked eyes and wet gaping mouth. Another blow and she bit into her hair. Her eyes were full of pain and remorse.

My heart was pounding. No one was looking at me. They had forgotten me for a moment. I tightened my legs together – again feeling the tension around the soft edges of my cunt. I remembered again my fear and my need to escape. It flooded over me. I clenched my fists, jumped up and ran for the door.

I was still pulling on my shirt as I ran out into the main office. Everything was a blur but I saw my passport, still sitting behind the desk. Without stopping, I reached over and grabbed it. I knocked over a large jar full of charity money. It smashed on the floor with a bang. Coins and dollar bills spread around my feet. I scooped up as much as I could and ran to the door.

They were behind me – the male officer hissing and barking, the sergeant baring his teeth and drooling spit in frothy streams down his chin. I grabbed a cord on one of the window blinds and yanked it hard. The light burst in – it was morning, the sun was already high. The sergeant stopped in his tracks, the male officer dropped to his knees. Spit bubbled from his mouth as he tried to shield his eyes from the light.

I released another blind. The sergeant and the officer clawed their way backwards towards the interview room. The beautiful woman was hanging on the peg, her hair still in her mouth, her eyes still soaked with tears. I just saw Pastor Wick in the darkness of the room before I pushed the door open and ran out into the street.

It was hot. I didn't even look behind. I jumped into the back of a waiting taxi and threw myself into the seat. I dragged at the hem of my short skirt as it rode up high on my thighs.

'Airport! Quick!' I shouted to the driver. 'As quick as you can!'

He looked in his mirror. I realised how dishevelled I was – I felt like a tramp. I opened my knees wider so that he could see the gleaming wetness of my naked cunt. It felt so good! I leant back and opened them more. I was filled with a need for relief.

I ran my hand down across my stomach until my fingers reached into the top of my crack. I felt comforted by their touch. My mind was filled with confusion. I needed to get away altogether. Just escaping from Pacific Heights was not enough. I needed to get out of the country. And I was not sure even that would be enough. I realised that although I had been cured of the pain of the day – the fear of light and need for the darkness – the lust was still within me. Although I was independent of the curse of the germ I carried within me, I could not resist the desire for blood that it brought with it.

I slipped my fingers into the wet flesh of my cunt and dropped my head back on the taxi seat. My heart pounded with excitement as the taxi pulled into a dingy alley and stopped. I drove my fingers deeper into the moist clinging flesh and waited for the release the driver would bring.

He climbed over the back of his seat and, without saying a word, turned me onto my front. He pulled up my skirt and exposed my wet cunt – squeezed between the tops of my thighs, glistening and expectant.

He smacked my bottom hard and I lifted myself to it, squirming under every blow as I sought out the stinging pain. He held my ankles wide as he drove his cock into my exposed anus. Spit ran from my mouth in sticky globs as he thrust me deeply in the rectum. He pulled it out and I sucked hard on his cock as his semen ran copiously from its end. I gulped it down and when I had swallowed it all, I turned onto my hands and knees again and begged for more.

2. THE BOX

The driver opened the door of the taxi and held out his hand, palm upwards, for a tip. I walked forward, hitched up my short skirt, and slid my cunt over his upturned hand, squeezing it against my wet flesh as I gripped its edges with the tops of my thighs. I licked his face, knowing I would never see him again, yet realising that the taste of his skin – the hide that protected his warm succulent blood – would remain forever in my mind. I pushed my face against his neck and pressed my teeth against it – just imagining biting into it filled my stomach with a wave of nervous excitement. I licked him again – a slow sloppy stroke of my tongue – this time running my lips along his throat as well. He did not know it but I was secretly offering him my germ, my ability to transform him into another kind – a form of existence that persisted beyond the light. I imagined my spit was his blood, rushing out of his veins and into my mouth – hot, spurting, filled with life and energy, nourishing, satisfying. I sucked it back, warm and glutinous, and tasted again his semen on my tongue. It was glorious! For a second I thought of his cock plugging my throat and how I had held it there as long as I could until finally, gasping for breath and with my body jerking and straining, I had pulled back and choked. I thought of how he had thrust it in again – not giving me time to get my breath back – and had driven it even deeper, forcing it in brutally as far as it would go. I thought of how I had choked and how he had kept it in, and I thought of how I had heaved and felt vomit somewhere deep in my gullet, and how I had felt his semen washing inside me, and the end of his cock expanding and pressing against the inside of my throat until, giddy and disoriented, I thought I would pass out.

I pressed a ten dollar bill into his still waiting and wet hand and left.

San Francisco International Airport terminal loomed above me; three long connected architectural waves – the Pacific swell in burnished steel. Inside it was frantic. Beautiful tanned women strode along confidently between down-and-out buskers, beggars and leftover hippies. Nobody took any notice of my tousled hair, ripped shirt and semen smeared face – I was just part of the incongruity, the absurdity of Southern California.

I felt as if I was caught in a dream. It was as though the surroundings in the airport were like my life – confused, polarized and ill-matched. Yes, it was as if everything must be a delusion – Pacific Heights, the execution of Father Dawson, the infection, the vampires and now the pursuing flock and Pastor Wick. It all seemed ridiculous. I would be locked up as insane if I told anyone, I thought. But it was true! I couldn't get away from it. I looked behind me, suddenly fearful of being followed. I was paranoid as well!

I went to the restroom. I stood in front of a brightly lit mirror and doused my face with water. A middle aged woman holding a small poodle in the crook of her arm came out of a cubicle and stood beside me. The dog barked at me as though it was startled. The woman looked me up and down haughtily and with disgust.

I stared at myself in the mirror. The two small puncture marks in my neck convinced me that even though everything seemed ridiculous, or fantastic, or unbelievable, there was no doubt about it – what I thought had happened, really had happened! I went cold as the undeniable realisation flooded over me. I saw my lips trembling and I shivered all over.

The dog barked again and the woman shielded its eyes, as if the sight of me somehow upset its sensitivity. I turned to it and exposed my teeth. It made a frightened bleating sound and curled up in the woman's protective arms.

I walked through the main concourse. The buff coloured surface of the shiny marble floor reflected the brightness of the lighting panels in the ceiling. I saw a tacky sign stuck at an angle over a glass door squeezed between a bureau de change and a fire exit: "Acme Couriers – worldwide non-registered couriers". Beneath it a white plaque hung on a chromium linked chain: "Couriers wanted – free travel". A tall dark haired woman walked away from the door into the concourse.

The door stuck as I tried to push it open. I looked around it.

It was a cramped room, stacked with boxes and envelopes. A man with a sallow complexion sat on the edge of a small desk holding the wrists of a frightened looking young woman who was sitting forward on a leather covered typist's chair. The man's black hair was slicked back and he had a small black moustache and a goatee beard. The young woman had a mane of tousled blonde hair and was wearing a short, red plaid skirt and a red blouse with a frilly white collar. She looked up at him enquiringly with wide blue eyes. She seemed sorry for something – unsure how to make good her mistake. Neither of them saw me peering around the door.

He poked his face towards her and shouted. She bit her lips fearfully.

'This is the last time you will make a mistake like this, Kristy. You've done it before and I have had to discipline you. And now you've done it again! Sometimes I think you want me to punish you! I can't let this pass, you know that, Kristy. You know that don't you?'

Kristy bit her lips. Her eyes were tearful but she kept looking at him, as if her suppliant gaze would somehow save her from chastisement.

'I'm so sorry,' she said falteringly. 'So, so sorry. It won't happen again, sir. I promise. It really won't happen again.'

'I know you think that, Kristy, but I must make sure. If we lose much more business we'll both be out of a job. And what then?'

Kristy dropped her gaze. It was as if she was at last admitting her mistake and now acknowledging she must be punished for it. Her hair fell forward around her flushed cheeks.

I clung to the edge of the door-frame. I could not take my eyes from the scene inside the room.

'You know what to do, Kristy.'

'Yes, sir, I know.'

He let go of her wrists. For a second she sat back on the typist's chair. She opened her mouth and licked the tip of her tongue across the edges of her bottom teeth. I could see how white they were – perfect Californian teeth. She took a deep breath – her pert breasts rose, her taut cleavage deepened. She looked like a homecoming queen, or a vibrant cheerleader – athletic, tanned, physical, and filled with youthful sexuality.

He nodded as if to prompt her.

She twisted sideways on the chair and stood up. Her waist was narrow and the taut curve of her buttocks pressed out beneath her short tartan skirt. She looked at him again, this time for permission, and again he nodded.

He stood up from the desk. On it there was a heavy black typewriter and on the left hand side a pile of white paper. She moved the typewriter slightly and tidied the paper – neatening the edges of the pile, making sure it was symmetrically placed alongside the typewriter. She opened a drawer in the desk and removed a long wooden ruler. She placed it neatly on the right hand side of the typewriter.

She stood back from the table and bent forward at a right angle. She rested her elbows on the table. She was not wearing any panties. I could just see the tops of her thighs where they joined the base of her rounded buttocks. Between them I could make out the thin line of her crack, squeezed between the perfect oval created by the delectable raised edges of her soft pink cunt. A thrill of excitement passed through my stomach. My hips ached and I felt my nipples hardening and pressing against the material of my shirt.

Kristy waited, not moving.

Suddenly the man spoke in an everyday tone.

'Kristy. Type out a new courier order. It's for a package to Rome. It must go today.'

Still leaning forward on her elbows Kristy took a sheet of paper from the pile on the left of the typewriter and wound it into the heavy black carriage. She cranked the wheel on the side and pulled it through until it reappeared and jutted upwards. She dropped the chromium carriage guard back with a metallic snap.

She bit her lips and began to type.

It was difficult for her, leaning forward while trying to hit the heavy keys with enough force to make them work. Suddenly two of the keys jammed together. She stopped immediately, looked sideways and bit onto her lips nervously.

'Oh, Kristy. Another mistake. This is not good enough. I must teach you to do your work better. You understand don't you?'

'Yes, yes I do.'

'Good! Hand me the ruler.'

She passed him the wooden ruler. He held its ends, flexed it, then rubbed its smooth surface against the palm of his left hand.

'And prepare yourself!'

Kristy reached back with both hands and took hold of the hem of her tartan skirt. She raised it slowly, bit by bit completely exposing her naked bottom.

I stared at the shape of her buttocks and the delectable oval of her cunt. A thrilling wave of excitement passed through me. I ran my hand between my legs, unable to resist the softness of my own aching flesh. I pulled my fingers between the lips. The slit was wet and opened easily. The tips of my fingers slid in and I pressed them deeply so that my clitoris rested against the inside of my hand. I felt its throbbing heat and another thrill ran through me in a shimmering wave.

The man flexed the ruler again. I could see the tension in it – its springiness, its tautness, its ability to deliver stinging pain.

'Now, Kristy, you must learn not to make any more mistakes with your typing. Do you understand?'

'Yes, I understand.'

'And why must you not make any mistakes?'

'Because we will be out of work.'

'Good. And to help you not make any mistakes, what must I do?'

'You must punish me if ever I make one.'

'And will you learn from this?'

'Yes, yes I will.'

'And have you been punished before for making mistakes?

'Yes, yes I have.'

'And so why do I have to punish you again?'

'Because I have not learned from my punishment.'

'So what must I do?'

'You must punish me harder. Every time I make another mistake my punishment must be harder, more painful.'

'And will you learn from this?'

'Yes, yes sir, I will.'

'And if you don't?'

'Then you must keep punishing me even harder.'

'Good. Make sure your skirt stays where it is, then you may rest on your elbows on the desk. Do not look away from the mistake you have made on the typing paper in the typewriter. That is how you will learn, seeing your mistake as you feel the pain of your punishment. Your error will become etched in your mind by the pain and you will learn to do better.'

Kristy folded the edge of the hem of her skirt into the waistband so that it would stay in place, then she put her elbows on the table as he had instructed.

'Look at your mistake!'

She stared at the page in the typewriter.

He turned his left shoulder towards her as he drew back the long ruler in his right hand.

'Look at your mistake! Do not take your eyes from it!'

He held the ruler high in the air for a moment – lining up the path it must travel, fixing the place across the midpoint of her buttocks where he intended the blow to land – then, with only one thing in mind, he brought it down hard.

I felt my jaw dropping. I felt myself gaping. I could not move. I was fixed to the spot – waiting for the ruler to make contact, waiting to hear the smacking crack as it bit into her skin, waiting to see it come away as it sprang against the tautness of her buttocks, waiting to see the red line that it left. Yes, I wanted to see. I wanted to see how red the stripe would be, how angry, how long, how it would follow the curves of her bottom. And I wanted to hear her scream. I wanted to hear her pain. I wanted to feel it vibrating in my head as she released it. I was drawn into what she would suffer, soaked up by it, absorbed by the pain she would feel at his hands.

It was as if it was all happening in a strange slow motion, and in silence. I heard nothing as the surface of the ruler touched her skin. I saw no movement as it sprang back slowly. It was as of the world had frozen around me, as if no signals were getting through to me and yet still change was going on. Then suddenly, like an explosion it all happened. I saw the flashing descent of the ruler, I heard its swish. I felt the panic within me as it approached. I saw it hit her skin, and flex against it. I watched it come away as her taut bottom sprang against it. I saw the instant red line it left. And as quickly I heard her scream, like an animal – primitive, penetrating, filled only with suffering. And I saw Kristy desperate to keep her elbows on the table, afraid to move, afraid to disobey the orders she had been given, afraid to take her eyes off the mistake she had made, afraid in case she had as yet learned nothing.

'Will you make the same mistake again?'

'No...No...No...'

I saw the ruler being lifted again. I saw it waiting in the air, waiting from the command of its master, waiting for the command to his limbs to bring it down, to deliver her lesson.

'I don't believe you!'

It came down again – noiseless again, frozen in time yet still passing through it, silent yet storing up its explosive crescendo.

I saw her tense as it struck – like a stiff board – then the wait as the earth caught up, then the screech and the release of all that had been held back, then she was fluid again and she writhed in agony.

Another red stripe, another welt, another punishing sting another expectation of more.

'And now, have you learned your lesson?'

'Yes...Yes...Yes...'

Her voice was already frail, shaking, wavering, fearful.

'Yes, I have learned my lesson. I will never make the same – '

The ruler came down again before she could finish. It struck her with a loud cracking smack. I saw it catch the delightful oval of her cunt, slicing across it, making her tense in supreme anguish, writhing and struggling to stay in position so that she could face up to her misdemeanour and learn from her punishment.

I pushed my fingers deeper into my wet cunt. I hung onto the door-frame with my other hand – moaning, drooling, completely engrossed.

'And now, have you learned your lesson now?'

'I have, yes, I – '

Another smacking blow, another scream, another cut across her tender naked flesh, another apology, another doubt, another cutting stroke, another howling scream.

I bent forward to allow my fingers in deeper. I felt something behind me – heat, pressure, another body!

'Like looking eh?' said a man's voice.

I was startled and half turned. A man in a courier uniform was standing right behind me.

'Like looking, eh?' he repeated.

All I could see in my mind was the red stripes on Kristy's buttocks and cunt. All I could hear in my head were her howling shrieks. All I could feel were my fingers still delving deeply inside my wet cunt and my clitoris pounding against the palm of my thrusting hand.

The man smiled I think – I wasn't sure, I didn't care. I was too overwhelmed with the images and sounds of Kristy's punishment – I was reeling with them. I saw the man's neck, exposed above his white collar. I saw the blue veins and I saw the pounding artery running up to beneath the point of his jaw. I did not think, or pause. I did not consider my action or work out an approach.

I did not think of the consequences. I heard the ruler smacking down again and I launched myself at him, my mouth open, my teeth bared; the sight of his neck and its veins the only thing in my mind.

I heard myself growling, I think, again I was not sure. I felt as if an animal inside me had been released. I smelled his skin. I heard his blood pulsating. Yes, I certainly heard that. And I knew that all I wanted was to taste it. I felt my open mouth making contact. I felt my teeth against his skin. I felt them biting – the tension against the flesh, the slow giving away of the weaker to the stronger, the sense of tearing.

He tried to shake me off – like someone would defend themselves against a stinging bee. I clawed at him. Overcome with eagerness and need. He lashed out at me in a sudden panic. He shouted and kicked and I growled and slobbered. He knocked me to the ground.

Suddenly I was on the floor – the cool marble tiles against my naked buttocks, my legs shaking, my heart pounding, frothing spit running in a stream from my gaping mouth. I bared my teeth at him. I wanted to leap to my feet and lurch at him again. I felt he was my prey and I would not be stopped in my pursuit of him.

He looked down at me. I saw his face whiten with terror. I saw a realisation come over him – he was faced with something which terrified him. Me!

The man ran off. A small crowd gathered around me. I couldn't get up – I felt so weak. I felt someone reaching down and taking my hand. It was the man with the goatee beard from the courier's office.

'It's okay,' he said to the people who had gathered around. 'No panic, she's just fainted. She'll be alright after a sit down. No problem. It's all over. Nothing to see.'

He helped me into the office. I was shaking all over.

'Here, sit down, sit down,' he said as if nothing had

happened. 'You don't know how lucky you are. I've got just the job for you. You could say it's been waiting for you all your life – it's just perfect. Kristy! Bring the box! Kristy!'

My head was swimming. Only minutes ago I had been watching Kristy being punished, I had heard her screaming for mercy, and now she was putting something down on the table as cool as could be. And the man outside. He had run away as if he'd seen a demon. I had wanted so much to taste his blood. I couldn't believe what had come over me. I had been completely out of control. The thought made me shiver. I went cold. Had I lost control of myself? Was I under the same spell as the flock? Was I a demon?

Kristy placed a white box on the table between us. She looked under her eyes at me and tried to smile. I could see she was finding it difficult to keep back her tears. I couldn't believe how everything seemed to have returned to normal, as though what I had witnessed had not happened. I wanted to run my hands up her short tartan skirt and feel the welts on her bottom – just to be sure my memory wasn't playing tricks.

'Sit down. Sit down,' said the man launching into a well tried sale patter. 'There on the table, right in front of your eyes, is your passport to freedom. What's your name?'

'Syra.'

'Syra, just think of it, passage to a new world. For a few days of your time and enough money to change your whole life! Syra I am the answer to your prayer. Can you believe your fortune?'

I looked at the box. It was red plastic with a white top and a red carrying handle. On the side was a white circle with a red cross in the centre. Below the circle against a rectangular white background it said in red capitals "HUMAN ORGAN".

I pulled back as I read it.

'Nothing to worry about,' said the man. 'We've all got them. Just think of it as your new life. Just pick up the box and you're on the way.'

'I don't understand.'

'It's simple. This box needs delivering to Bratislava. You take it on a plane, make sure it gets to the address I will give you and that's it. *No problemo*. They'll pay you on delivery. Enough for you to fly on anywhere in the world. It's so easy. I really envy you. What a way to travel, eh? You'll be part of the jet set.'

'Is that all I have to do?'

'It sure is, Syra. Just make sure you deliver the package at the right place at the right time. Pick up your money and on you go. It's that simple.'

'What do people want with this, this "human organ"?'

'I can't say. What I can say is that if you can imagine it then somebody's doing it, and if you can't imagine it, then somebody's doing that as well!'

He laughed loudly at his insight – it was obviously a well tried aphorism.

It seemed easy – ridiculously easy. There must be a catch. But why should there be? Why not? I thought, Europe again, away from the USA, away from the flock. Yes, he's right! I could start a new life. Things would be different there. I could be free at last. My concerns suddenly turned to resolve.

'How soon can I go?'

I'd said it, I'd made a commitment. I was going to change my life at last!

'If you've got your passport, you can be on the next flight. It's a dream ticket! Here, Syra, welcome to the staff of Acme Couriers!'

3. MIRANDA

It felt a bit odd at first – carrying the box – quite a few people stared at it inquisitively, but I soon got used to it. I thought some of them recognised me from the incident outside the Acme Couriers office, but I wasn't sure. I know I still looked dishevelled, but I didn't care. I felt excited about the journey, looking forward to something new, leaving the terrors of the past behind.

I checked in – I'd got a couple of hours to wait. I sat on a spare seat at the "Firewood Grill". I rested the box on my knees as I stared at a group of men eating barbecued steak on long steel skewers. The red-brown sauce dripped down their chins. One of them stared at me, pushed his hand down the front of his trousers and massaged his cock. I got out my ticket: San Francisco to London. The man at Acme Couriers had given me a note to present at the airline desk for the flight from London to Bratislava. A wave of excitement ran through my stomach. I could hardly believe it!

The tall woman with short black hair I had seen leaving the courier's office sat down opposite. She was poised and graceful. She opened a laptop and began tapping the keys with her long red fingernails. She was elegantly dressed in a black suit, white shirt and black tie. She wore tight fitting black leather boots that ended mid calf. Her tight fitting skirt was slit at the side and its hem reached to the tops of her boots. She did not look up and so I stared all the more. There was a name on the lid of the laptop. It was upside down and I struggled to read it. In the end I made it out – "Miranda". It sounded like the name of a Greek goddess. She suited it perfectly.

Miranda took a deep breath, closed the lid of her laptop and sat staring ahead. She looked pensive, as though contemplating a task that she had undertaken many times before. She smiled at me fleetingly, got up and went to the restroom. She was very composed and certain – placing her toes forward before letting them touch the ground, allowing her arms to hang freely at her sides, keeping her shoulders well back and her chin high. And she only looked where she was going. That was what struck me most of all. She did not look to the side, nor at anyone else, she was in no way distracted from her purpose – she just looked straight ahead, her mission the only thing on her mind, her focus only on her task. Miranda, I thought, what a beautiful name.

She stopped for a second at the entrance to the restrooms, looked back for a moment then went inside. I felt a wave of excitement in my stomach. I knew she had smiled at me, beckoned me, I thought. It had only been brief but I knew she was inviting me to follow. Yes, of course, she wanted me to follow her!

I couldn't resist it. I got up and walked after her.

I had only gone a few steps when I realised I had forgotten the box! I turned back in a panic. It was sitting on the leather covered seat where I had left it! I rushed back and grabbed it. My heart was pounding. I felt foolish and ridiculous. A security guard walked past and frowned. I imagined him thinking I had stolen it and I felt a flushing heat on my face. I hurried towards the restroom. I knew my cheeks were red with embarrassment and that fuelled in me an undirected sense of shame.

It was echoey inside the restrooms – the same buffed marble flooring as the rest of the building glittered around my feet. The walls were covered in sterile, shiny white tiles with a band of black ones at waist height. It smelled of neroli and ylang ylang – sharp and lemony, spicy and refreshing. Even the aroma seemed to be bright beneath the harsh white lights.

I stopped near the right angled entrance. I could hear voices inside – one smooth and cultured, the other younger, Mexican, eager to please. Ensuring I could not be seen by whoever was on the other side, I looked around the edge of the entrance. It was Miranda. She was talking to a young Mexican girl – a cleaner in a blue overall.

'You take the money...and keep the change...be quick...remember...really cold.'

I couldn't hear everything Miranda said. She pressed some dollar bills into the girl's hand. The girl smiled, stuffed the money into the breast pocket of her overall and started to walk to the entrance.

I dodged back into the main concourse and stood behind a red and black ice machine.

The young Mexican girl emerged, mopping the floor absently. She was obviously pretending to do her job while having something else more important on her mind. She half looked up but as soon as I caught her eye she looked down quickly. Her lips were full and pouting. Her breasts were compact and pulled in tightly beneath her light blue overall. I could see that her nipples were hard and pressing out against the thin material. I imagined sucking them. How sweet I thought they would be – springy, youthful and perfectly formed. She rolled the tip of her tongue along her top lip. It glistened in the harsh bright light. I thought of her young wet cunt and imagined my tongue slipping along its moist crack. For a moment I tasted it and when I breathed in I inhaled again its delicate scent.

She worked her way towards a man who was standing nearby carrying a briefcase. She started speaking to him. He nodded earnestly. She took out some of the money from her overall and pushed it quickly into his hand. He nodded again. Knowing she was distracted, I moved back into the entrance. She didn't see me. I waited for a moment as the ice machine churned out an avalanche of fresh ice then I went inside.

I could see the door to one of the cubicles was closed. Miranda must be in there, I thought. I went into the next one and closed the door behind me.

For a few moments there was no sound. Then I heard footsteps on the tiled floor – a man's footsteps!

I put the box on the floor, held my breath and waited. It was ridiculous but I couldn't stop myself – and now I was committed, trapped!

The man stopped at the door of the cubicle Miranda was in. He knocked softly on the thin metal door.

'Yes?'

'Are you waiting for me?' he asked.

'Yes.'

Miranda's voice was so cultured, so succinct, so definite. The door opened.

I climbed up onto the pedestal seat and peeped over the top of the shiny stainless steel partition. Miranda was kneeling on the floor, her arms draped around the white WC pedestal.

'Come in,' she said to the man without looking around.

The man stood in the open doorway and looked down at her. Her rounded bottom was tight inside her dark grey skirt. Her hips curved delectably from her narrow waist. Her suit jacket had ridden up slightly to reveal her white shirt. It had two hand sewn seams down the back. Her long shiny red lacquered nails looked like pools of blood against the vitreous white of the WC as she clung to it.

'I will start like this first,' said the man.

'Yes.'

He reached down and undid the long side zip of her skirt. He pulled the skirt down and left it around the backs of her knees. She was wearing black satin panties – high cut and pulled smoothly across the taut skin of her buttocks. A black suspender belt and black sheer stockings contrasted with her pale smooth skin.

She did not move.

The man stroked the smooth of his hand across the satin surface of her panties. He pressed his finger between her legs and squeezed the flesh of her cunt. I could see how pliable and soft it was. I imagined my lips against it, my tongue licking in its groove. As he drew his finger away it left a slight indent that ran along the length of her crack. I wanted so much to lick along it, to lick the material and feel the gentle notch in it as it was pressed firmly against the delectable slit that ran beneath it. My heart started to beat faster.

Still she did not move.

He opened his briefcase and drew out a shiny black leather flogger – a braided handled scourge with at least twenty or thirty thin leather tails. He draped the heavy tails across his hand – they fell in a soft curve, wrapping themselves around the edge of his hand, caressing it, stroking it as if inviting it to lead them to the tight pulled material of her panties.

Still she did not move.

'I will begin,' he said.

'Yes.'

He flicked the whip a couple of times across the palm of his hand, letting it get the taste for flesh. Satisfied, he knelt behind Miranda, drew the whip back and brought it down across her panty covered bottom.

I heard her draw breath – a short sharp inhalation – but I did not see her flinch or pull away. He brought it down again. It slapped against her skin – smoothly following the line of her curved buttocks. Again I heard her suck in air. He pulled the whip away. A broad redness appeared on the sides of her bottom where they were not covered by her silky panties. Again it came down – swishing, hard, firm. He set up a tempo – pulling back, waiting for a moment, bringing it down, making contact, holding the flogger's flails against her skin, removing it to reveal its blotched red mark before bringing it down again.

I realised I was pushing myself rhythmically against the partition – pressing my mouth against its edge, my breasts against its surface in time with the lashing that was being inflicted on Miranda.

'It will have to be harder,' said the man.

'Yes.'

'And more painful.'

'Yes.'

He reached down and took hold of the waistband of her black panties. He pulled them down slowly, not stopping when the gusset stuck to the sticky wetness of her cunt or its edges clung to the insides of her thighs. He dragged them to her knees and left them there. Where they had covered her bottom the redness was less than it was where her skin had been exposed. The crack between her buttocks was tight and precise. I could not see between them and could only imagine the flesh of her cunt – squeezed up, succulent, soft and yielding. The picture in my mind filled me with a surge of pleasurable heat in my own cunt. I gave a sudden gasp.

He brought it down again. This time she flinched as the tails found the exposed flesh of her cunt. I took the edge of the partition between my lips. Its harsh coolness inflamed me and I gripped it between my teeth; they grated against the unforgiving steel.

'Lift it higher,' he said.

It was a straightforward command, given coldly.

'Yes.'

Her tone excited me – so clear-cut and matter of fact.

She dropped her face lower into the WC bowl – her hair spread along its edges, her arms folded around its base. She kept her bottom high.

The lash came down again. This time she flinched, she had lifted her bottom higher just as the whip came down, exposing her cunt and making its flesh available to the cutting flails of the swishing whip.

Now I saw the slit at the centre of her flesh – precise and glistening, exposed, unprotected, tender and vulnerable.

Spit was running from my mouth. I gripped the steel edge of the partition hard between my teeth, its metallic sterility made me drool even more. I inhaled its harshness – pure, inorganic, lifeless. I thought I could stay there forever – watching the flails coming down on Miranda's buttocks, watching them redden, watching her flinch, watching the glistening wet crack of her cunt exposed to the angry smacking leather.

'Higher.'

Still the cold tone.

'Yes.'

Still the matter of fact response.

She dropped her face lower into the bowl and lifted her bottom as high as she could. I could see her cunt clearly now – reddened by the flail, wet, perfectly formed.

This time when the whip came down Miranda twisted in pain. She could no longer remain still – the pain was too much to bear. Again and she twisted so much she buried her head down into the bowl and I heard her choke and splutter as her face dipped into the water at its base.

He did not stop – harder and harder, faster and faster, more and more pain delivered in the swishing tails of the tightly gripped whip.

I pressed my nipples against the stainless steel partition – they were so hard and aching. I slobbered and drooled. I felt the edges of my teeth against the metal. I wanted to bite into it, to suck at it, to devour its inanimate lifelessness. I wanted to melt it with my heat so that I could drink it and quench my lustful thirst.

Miranda kept her bottom high even though she could no longer absorb the pain.

Suddenly he stopped. She went still. He reached into his briefcase and brought out a transparent polythene bag. It was filled with ice. He held it against the red smudged skin of her cunt. She tensed in shock and bent her back in a high contorting arch as the freezing ice made contact.

'Stay down!' he said, suddenly angered by her behaviour – her resistance, her independent action.

He pressed the ice bag hard against her flesh. Her buttocks tightened involuntarily as the coldness delivered a new pain – a contrasting pain, a different experience of suffering. He was displeased by her involuntary response – it seemed too much like disobedience. He scowled.

He pulled the ice filled bag away and continued the beating. Again he stopped and repeated the process – pressing the freezing bag of ice against her hot and agonised flesh. Unable to control her body to start with she tensed but, struggling against her body's involuntary reaction and using all her will power, she managed to make herself stop. He pressed it harder. She twisted in contorted anguish then again brought herself under control and remained still. I could see she was filled with the burning of heat and overcome with the freezing pain of ice. I could see it was barely tolerable.

I realised I was licking the bare shiny metal of the partition – stroking my wet salivating tongue against it, pressing the flat of its flesh against its smooth gleaming surface.

Miranda was clinging desperately to the WC; her groans and cries echoing against the vitreous material of the inside of the bowl. I wanted to crawl over the partition, to take her place, to feel the heat of the lashing whip against my cunt, to feel the freezing pain of the ice as it was pressed against its soft flesh. I wanted to feel the intolerability of it all. The thought of it! I imagined my cunt stinging, I imagined myself wincing, unable to protect myself, no longer in charge of my body, clinging to the WC – a victim of the man's anger and strength, of my own lack of control, of my own seizures of delight.

He bore down on her viciously. I could see she was barely holding on – barely able to bring herself to stillness after she writhed in agony, barely able to recover enough to take the next agonising pain, barely able to stand the howling cries that echoed in her ears. He crushed the ice pack against her cunt – now laced with red lines from the lashing flogger that he wielded so cruelly. He pressed it flat against her burning flesh – squeezing it, setting it on fire with its coldness, confusing her senses and throwing her into turmoil.

I watched my spit running down the other side of the stainless steel partition. It flowed from my mouth in a bubbling stream and glistened on the shiny surface as it traced its way towards the polished tiled floor.

I could not make out words in her cries, I was not sure what I thought I heard, what I imagined, but they drew me towards her. It was her pain, I think – her supplication, her inability to take it – and it sucked me in like a vortex. I could not hold back. I clawed over the top of the partition – bringing my knee up and lifting it over the edge. I thought she was crying for help, pleading for mercy, saying how sorry she was. I knew what I was doing, I knew I was exposing myself to goodness knows what but it didn't matter – I could not resist.

Suddenly, he turned and saw me. There was surprise on his face but anger as well – he was annoyed by my intrusion, enraged at being stopped. He threw the flogger down. Miranda sighed and flopped to the side; she must have thought her ordeal over. He reached up and grabbed me by the hair. He pulled me over the partition. The top edge scraped against my breasts, my nipples, the points of my hips and, as I twisted sideways and my legs opened, the crack of my cunt. I winced in pain as I fell giddily to the hard tiled floor on the opposite side of the partition. For a moment I thought I must have hurt myself, but I had not.

Miranda stayed where she was – on all fours, her arms wrapped around the WC pedestal. I bent over her – stretching my arms down on either side of her chest, straddling her hips with my widespread knees, raising my bottom like hers and pressing my hips down onto her. My cunt pressed against her red hot buttocks. My legs were so wide, my cunt so open. There was nothing else in my mind but the sweet expectation of punishment – painful punishment. I could think of nothing else. I knew he stood back – perhaps standing in the open doorway, I couldn't tell. I know he lifted the flogger, but I didn't hear its tails caressing each other or its movement cutting through the air. I know he waited for a while, but I couldn't tell how long – it felt like an eternity.

When it struck it was so much more painful than I had imagined. It felt as if the skin of my bottom was being ripped away. It was agony – complete, delectable agony. I yelped and pressed my cunt harder against Miranda's bottom. I did not try to protect myself from the flails of the leather whip. I did not bring my legs together or think of protecting the soft flesh of my exposed cunt. I lifted my bottom higher and I felt Miranda's bottom rise against me – rise with me. I waited for the next and felt it against my cunt. And the next and I cried out and yelped and pressed myself harder against Miranda as she pressed back and lifted me even higher against the reason for my pain.

I knew I would feel the ice but I did not know how long I would have to wait. When it came its coldness burned me even more than the heat of the flailing whip. It penetrated me to my core – filling me, stuffing me full of its freezing sting. I could not have anticipated what it would feel like – the contrast of the cold and the heat, of the ice and the fire, had been impossible to foresee. My mind was filled with light – there was no picture to put to it, no fantasy to identify it, no wish to fix to it; I was simply blinded by its blaze.

I felt my body tightening, relaxing, and tightening again. I know the heat of my cunt melted the ice that was pushed against me, but the wetness that dripped from my flesh was also from my flesh itself. I felt myself convulsing in spasms as the beating continued, and these jerking seizures were still gripping me, still tossing me about in the blinding white ether, when the next fire of ice was pressed against my tortured flesh.

I howled and twisted as the pain continued to inflict its delectable joy. I felt as if I was tumbling, dipping, sinking in a pure white world where there was no up nor down, no weight, no fixed point. I was captured by unknown forces in a delightful balance of suffering, sacrifice and pleasure.

He stopped. I don't know why – I didn't want him to, I knew that. I knew it was all over though. I slid from Miranda's back and lay beside her, propped against the cold stainless steel of the partition, hardly aware of its temperature and smoothness. Miranda's head was still in the WC bowl, but now I could see her face. Spit was running from her mouth, she was gasping for breath, her firm breasts were heaving, her eyes were wide and staring. I panted in time with my thumping heart – rapid, irregular, out of control.

Miranda's lips moved. Spit bubbled from them. They moved again. She was saying something – saying something to me.

'Go,' she said. 'Go. You have taken enough. There will be more, but it is for me.'

My heart was beating so fast, I could hardly speak. At last I managed to say something.

'No, I can't leave – '

'Go! Go! The rest is for me. You have taken enough. Go!'

She went silent, staring into the water in the WC bowl – vacuous, expectant, terrified.

I struggled to my feet. The man was standing with the flogger in his hand. He smiled. I pushed past him and ran out of the cubicle. I fell against one of the washbasins and had to steady myself. I stared into the mirror.

Beyond my flushed and spit smeared face I saw the Mexican girl still pushing her mop across the shiny tiled floor. She moved towards the cubicle. The man stood back as she pushed her wet mop around Miranda's body. Miranda didn't move, she just lay there clinging to the WC, panting, keeping her reddened bottom high, and waiting for the girl to leave so that her flogging could continue.

Suddenly, I saw the box sitting on the floor in the cubicle next to the one in which Miranda lay. I was gripped by a sense of overwhelming panic. It was my ticket out of here! I rushed into the cubicle, grabbed it and rushed out as fast as I could. Outside I leaned against the cold throbbing ice machine and shivered.

I went back to the "Firewood Grill". I could hardly sit down. I was sure people noticed. I thought they must have guessed what had been going on. Then I realised that was ridiculous!

I guzzled a coke. My bottom was so sore!

The next I knew an hour had passed and the last call for my flight was coming over the speaker system.

I rushed though the concourse with the box in my hand. Everyone stared – I knew they did. I nearly slipped over twice. The pretty girl at the gate checked my ticket and handed me back my boarding slip.

Breathlessly, I hurried down the jet-way. There was no one else to be seen! I ran as fast as I could. I was sure I was going to miss the plane! I tripped on one of the sliding joints in the floor and was thrown face forward to the ground. The box flew out of my hand and clattered round the corner in front of me. I jumped up and ran after it. The entrance to the plane was directly ahead. A stewardess was just picking up the box. She held it out towards me with a broad smile.

I turned back just to see if I had dropped anything else. Pastor Wick was coming down the jet way behind me! Where had he come from? How had he found me? I thrust my ticket into the stewardess's hand.

'You left it a bit late, sweetie. Another few seconds and we would have gone without you. "53A", all the way down, on the right. Please take your seat and get buckled up.'

As I turned past the entrance galley she pushed the door to. Its thud filled me with relief. I was safe! At last I was safe!

I pushed my way down the long aisle, still busy with passengers taking off their jackets and struggling to load the luggage lockers. I found my seat – right at the back. Miranda was sitting in "53B"!

4. FLIGHT 286

Miranda smiled as I sat down. She looked so calm and assured.

'Nice to make your acquaintance,' she said in a smooth melodic Californian accent. 'My name's Miranda.'

I was embarrassed and showed it.

'I'm Syra.'

We shook hands. Her skin felt like silk. Her nails clicked together as she drew her hand away. They made me think of teeth chattering in the cold.

'Don't be embarrassed.'

'I'm not really...just a bit flustered...rushing for the plane...I nearly missed it!'

'I hope you were delayed by something worthwhile.'

I felt my cheeks burning. She knew exactly why I was delayed! How could she be so calm?

'Yes...Yes, I was.'

My cheeks got even hotter. I wanted to sink into the seat and disappear.

'Good. Now, we've got a long journey together, so we had better make friends. Here, let me help you with your box.'

'No, it's fine. I'll put it up in the locker.'

I stood up, lifted the box and stretched to get it into the overhead compartment. It was already almost full and I couldn't get the box in. I stretched more, struggling to reach the back and trying to move some of the other bags and packages that cluttered it up. I stretched further. I knew my short skirt was riding up, I knew I wasn't wearing any panties and that my naked cunt must be in Miranda's full view, and I knew that my exposed bottom could be seen by any passenger behind me. I reached my hand back and pulled at the hem but it made little or no difference. I glanced at Miranda –

she was staring at my cunt. I had to reach sideways in the locker to wedge the box in and I opened my legs to balance myself. I knew she could see my exposed crack, and I knew she was looking at the glistening slit that ran along its centre.

'Do let me help,' she said unbuckling her seat belt and standing up as far as she could beneath the lockers. She faced me and reached up between my own outstretched arms. She pressed her breasts against mine – I could feel their heat, their firmness, the pointed harness of her nipples.

'This is Mandy your cabin staff supervisor speaking. I would like to welcome you to BA flight 286 from San Francisco to London Heathrow. I will be responsible for your in-flight comfort. If you have any requirements during the flight please do not hesitate to ask one of the cabin staff who will be only too pleased to help. For the moment, I would ask you all to take your seats and fasten your seat belts as we are taxiing to our take off runway.'

I strained to push the box into the locker. Miranda pushed harder against me. Now I could feel her hips against mine as she pressed against me. She squeezed her body hard against mine, turned sideways and pushed the box easily to the back of the locker. She turned back, smiled and kissed me fully on the mouth. Her lips were full and soft, satiny and warm. She opened them as she kissed me and I felt her probing tongue entering my mouth. She ran it along the insides of my lips, and then found my own tongue. I opened my mouth wide so that she could push it in as far as possible. It touched the back of my throat. I gagged slightly, but swallowed on it to allow it entry. It was so long!

She pulled away. For a moment her teeth touched mine – the hard contact sent a quivering thrill through me. I was left gaping, drooling, shivering with excitement.

She reached her hand down between my legs and pressed her fingers into the slit of my cunt. The wetness seemed to absorb them.

'See, we can be really good friends.'

She drew her hand away and sat back in her seat. I sat beside her. My hands were shaking as I tried to buckle up my belt.

'Here, let me help you. What are friends for?' She reached over to the belt buckle. She noticed her hand was wet from my cunt. 'Oops!' she said pulling a tissue from her bag and wiping her fingers. 'Silly me.'

I licked my lips as she did up my belt. I could still taste her tongue in my mouth. She pulled the metal clip together and yanked the belt tightly into it. I gasped as she pulled it tight.

'Too tight?'

'A bit, yes.'

'Better safe than sorry though, don't you think?'

'I suppose, yes.'

She was so refined and calm – so capable, unflappable. I felt silly in her presence, and yet being with her was comforting, reassuring – I felt looked after, strangely safe.

As we took off she started adjusting her watch.

'I always change my watch straightaway – it helps don't you think? With jet lag?'

I didn't have an opinion – I didn't have a watch! The realisation brought on the feeling of stupidity and embarrassment again. Yes, Miranda certainly had that affect on me and I felt my cheeks flush red as the thought passed through my mind.

We had only been going an hour or so and it began to get dark. We were served a meal – Miranda had the vegetarian option, I ate what I was given. I looked out of the window. The ground below became increasingly barren as we headed out across the northern wastelands towards the land of ice.

'I suppose you're wondering how I came to be in the restroom? How I came to be in the situation in which you found me? Have your been wondering, Syra? You haven't mentioned it, but I think I know. Am I right?'

Everything she said or did caught me off balance. I couldn't get over how cool she was, and how direct.

'Well, yes, I had really...'

I felt the flush of embarrassment coming over my cheeks again.

'Oh, Syra,' she said smiling and dabbing her lips with a tissue. 'Don't feel embarrassed. Here, you can have my sweet and I'll tell you.'

She pushed an apple tart and cream onto my tray. I picked it up and took a bite. Some of the cream stuck to my lips. I licked it away as she watched me.

'It was a few years ago, now – three or four, I suppose. I met him at a meeting, one of those "change your life" things, you know. He was one of the leaders, said he wanted to start his own religion. A bit ambitious, I thought. Anyway, we hit it off – really well. Actually, it was fantastic. I'd never known anything like it. He had some really strange ideas about treating me in certain ways – as a slave, shut up in boxes or cupboards, exposed in front of his friends, or strangers! He said that doing as he asked was a way of exploring my own feelings to the full. He was right. It was amazing!'

Her eyes widened as she began to talk about her life. The young red haired chief stewardess – Mandy – took our trays. I pushed up my seat back tray, turned to Miranda and settled back to listen. I pulled a dark blue fleece blanket over my knees. It was almost completely dark outside now. I saw some flashes of whiteness – the ice of the Arctic – then they were gone.

'I enjoyed following his orders,' Miranda continued. 'There was something strangely compelling about it. It never felt as if I was just "doing as I was told" – that's different. I was never compelled; although I never had any choice either. That's odd don't you think? I revelled in it, doing what he said. I suppose it was my commitment that made it so exciting, and the things he told me to do, of course. He never held back, never hesitated or disguised his intentions. "Stay here until I come and tell you otherwise" he would say. That was common to start with. I suppose he was testing me right from the start? Yes, maybe he was always testing me out? He never repeated a command. Once was enough. The first time, he left me in a room with a desk and chair, told me to stand behind the desk and wait until he returned. He was away for hours. I wasn't sure that time if I should sit or not. He hadn't told me to do either, so I didn't do anything. I just stood behind the desk waiting. I thought I might rest my hands on the desk when I felt tired or a bit dizzy but again, he hadn't said, so I didn't.'

'What happened when he came back?'

'He walked around me first, looking me up and down. I didn't move. He took out a ruler and measured the distance between the front of my slit and the edge of the table. Then he went away again and left me. He never said a word.'

I was captivated by her story. I pulled my knees up and wedged my feet against the back of the seat in front. I knew that if I opened my knees a bit she would be able to see my cunt. My stomach filled with anxious excitement at the thought.

'What next? What happened next?'

'I don't know how long it was – longer than the first time, I think. I stared at the door all the time. I know I was swaying back and forth, but I couldn't stop myself without putting my hands on the table and I didn't dare do that.'

'And when he came back, what did he do?'

'He stood in the doorway for a while. I was sure I was still swaying. I couldn't stop worrying that I had done something wrong. He walked around me again, checking me like before, and then he brought out the ruler and took the measurement again. He frowned and smacked the ruler across the palm of his hand. "You have moved. Only slightly, I admit, but it is measurable. I am not disappointed with you, this is your first task, but clearly there must be punishment. It is the only way to consolidate positive learning."

'I remained standing, hoping that I could remain still, hoping that the gap between the front of my cunt and the edge of the table did not widen or diminish, hoping he would not decide to take a further measurement. "It is appropriate that the punishment is simple and inflicted by the means of detecting your fault. And it is only a fault. Do not think you have let yourself down. It is an error from which you can learn. And, if you know you are learning, you will more easily be able to make your target perfection. Ah, perfection! Move forward, reach out and slide your hands to the opposite side of the table as you bend over. Feel the smoothness of the table top against the palms of your hands."

'I was wearing a grey skirt, a black suspender belt, black stockings and black silk panties. I had been wearing a jacket but he had told me to take it off when we had entered the room. He had hung it on a hanger and hung that on the back of the door. I did as he said. It was strange doing exactly as he had ordered, but I was strangely compelled. I wanted to do what he said so much – it was my only need; to carry out his orders, that's all I wanted to do. I closed my eyes as I reached my hands across the desk – I couldn't keep them open, my body was overcome with excitement. I grasped the opposite edge of the table and waited. Again, I don't know how long I stayed like that. I didn't hear him walk out, or walk around me, or move at all. For all I know it could have been an hour, or longer; it was impossible to tell.

'The next thing that happened was that I felt him lifting the hem of my skirt. He pulled it up so that it rested against the waistband. I knew how exposed I was to him. I knew my cunt was hot. I knew it was getting wet just at the thought of him looking at me. I could see in my mind my bottom covered with the black silky panties, the contrasting lines of the suspender belt and stockings against the paleness of my skin, and I could see his eyes feasting on it all.

'He pulled my panties down slowly, drawing the material against my skin, letting the gusset cling to my wet cunt as it dragged at its soft edges and pulled at my sensitive flesh. Finally, he pulled them all the way down to my ankles. Now I felt completely exposed. I wanted to lift my bottom higher so that he could see the oval of my cunt, so that when he brought the ruler down it would find the tautest of targets, but he had not said that I could move and so I stayed where he had instructed me.

'I sensed something before I felt the ruler making contact. Maybe it was a movement of the air that went ahead of it, maybe it was his hot breath, maybe it was an involuntary move I made and was not aware of – I could not tell, but I felt something. Then it struck – a hard smacking crack. It stung so much! It was so sharp and penetrating – so intense, so burning, so stinging. And again it came down – so rapidly after the first. He gave me no time to recover, no time to know if I had allowed myself to inadvertently flinch.

'In the end I couldn't help shying away, tightening as it struck – it was impossible not to, and he allowed it. And he allowed me first to moan, then to cry out, and then to shriek, and finally to howl. He did not stop me from showing my delight at pain, and he never has. He says it is essential for the positive learning process – to "express your transition to knowledge from pain" as he put it.

'After he had finished – after he had listened to my shrieking cries and seen that my bottom and the back of my thighs were sufficiently red – he took the ruler and left. He did not speak, did not give me any further instruction, just left in complete silence.

'I waited, spit running from my mouth, tears dripping like rain from my eyes.

'A girl who lived with him came to me in the end, pulled up my panties, pulled down my skirt and helped me to lie down on the floor. She gave me a blanket and later brought me a drink of water. That's how things carried on – following his instructions exactly, learning never to get anything wrong, being punished so that I could learn to get things right, being taken care of and prepared again for my next lesson in obedience.'

'What other things did you have to do?'

'Syra, I never *had* to do them I *wanted* to do them. It was my only wish in the world. I could have left him at any time. I was not a prisoner or a captive.'

I felt rebuked for not understanding her.

'Sorry,' I said and opened my knees a little so that she could see easily between my thighs.

'As I learned to follow his orders more precisely, so the tests he set me became more difficult. He did not push me too fast, or overstretch me though. Each stage was carefully regulated – a small mistake or error was punished harshly and this led to a further test and less errors. It was a marvellous regime. I woke every morning waiting for the next instruction, wondering if he considered me ready to move onto the next stage or if I was to be punished for previous error and retested. To start with a lot of it was standing, or leaning over, but soon it became even more physically challenging – having to fit into different small spaces, boxes and cupboards, all manner of confined places. By a careful introduction of new situations he made it easy for me in the beginning, I know that now, but at the time everything seemed a huge challenge. It was really hard to be cramped up in a trunk or a box, not daring to move, not knowing when he would come to assess how well I had done.

'And I saw him less and less. At first it troubled me – not having direct contact with him – but soon I learned that it was not necessary. All that mattered were his instructions and that I learned to carry them out. Sometimes he punished me himself to correct minor faults in my behaviour, sometimes – and increasingly more often – he sent someone else to punish me.

'The first time this happened I received a note to tell me to go to an alley off a dingy part of Nineteenth Street in the Castro district of San Francisco – not very salubrious. It said to face the wall next to a dumpster with a green and yellow "WM" on the side, lift the back of my skirt and pull my panties down. I went to the place as the instruction said – it was easy to find. A couple of winos drank from brown paper bagged bottles nearby. It was dirty and horrible. I faced the wall but when I started to lift my skirt I felt ridiculous and frightened. I couldn't see anyone else around and the idea of waiting, exposing my bottom like that, seemed absurd. For a moment, I couldn't believe that I had found myself there, in that position. Then suddenly, I lifted my skirt a bit higher. It was as though something more powerful was in control of me – and it felt so good! I couldn't believe it! I draped the hem on my waist; bending forward in that dirty alley, my panty-covered bottom exposed, not knowing who or when someone might come to me, or indeed if anyone would come. It was so exciting, so thrilling. I pulled my panties down a little but I couldn't continue. I was seized, frozen with pleasure; my cunt was wet, my nipples hard and throbbing, a deep aching gripped me between my hips. I felt a surge of joy – I don't know where it started, but it took my breath away. I felt giddy. I gulped for air. I tried to swallow but my throat was so dry it was impossible. I pressed my forearms hard against the damp brick wall and tightened my buttocks. I reached around and tried to pull my panties right down. My hands were shaking so much I couldn't even get a grip on them. Another surge of pleasure ran through me. My head reeled. I knew my bottom was exposed – somehow I had pulled my panties down. But even then I wasn't completely sure. It was only when I felt the slapping smack of a punishing flat hand against my taut skin that I realised it had truly happened.

'I never looked around. I clawed against the wall – scraping my fingernails against its rough graffiti-covered surface. My orgasm ran through me like a tide as the hand smacked my taut skin and drove me into excess after excess of delight. I slobbered and moaned. I cried out and howled. I felt the moisture of my cunt on the insides of my thighs, but still I never looked around. I never saw who it was – I did not want to know; it was a punishment carried out under his instruction, and that was all that mattered.

'Sometime after it had stopped I slumped to my knees. I felt my mouth being prised open and a hot cock being pushed in between my lips. I sucked until the end swelled against the insides of my cheeks and my mouth was filled with semen. Then there was another and I did the same. Semen dripped down my chin and onto my shirt and tie. I scraped it up with my fingers after they had gone and licked them until they were dry. I stayed there, on my knees, covered in semen shivering every so often with another surge of delight.

'I didn't leave until it was getting light – I wanted to be sure he had no more instructions for me. I felt dishevelled as I walked down Guerrero Street. Passers-by stared and some made remarks – "Tart! Whore! Bitch!". I didn't hear from him for a week and when I did I knew he was pleased with me because my next instruction was to carry out something completely different.

'He kept me shut up in a box for two whole days. He fed me through a straw that he poked through a hole in the side of the box. Sometimes I could hardly breathe, and I got spasms of cramp in my neck and legs. Another time he kept me naked in a wardrobe in a hotel room. I had to stand well inside behind some clothes hanging from a rail. He said I was not to move no matter what happened. Different guests used the room while I was in there and every time they opened the wardrobe I was overcome with a surge of ecstasy that made me so giddy and disorientated that I had to hold onto the rail to prevent myself from falling. One of the guests found me hanging onto the rail. Dragged me out, whipped me with his belt then told me to go back inside.

'Sometime after that I had a note from him saying that he believed I would now carry out any instruction he gave me perfectly. I lay back on my bed, pulled my panties down and plunged my fingers into my naked wet cunt. I pinched my clitoris and pulled it until I could hardly stand the pain. When finally I thought I could stand it no longer I lifted my hips up in a massive burst of howling joy. It was incredible – like winning a great prize or receiving an award. I picked the note up in my mouth and sucked at it. I dropped it then licked at it. I got onto all fours and lifted my bottom up as high as I could as I imagined him whipping me, bringing me to perfection, punishing my errors and shaping me into his faultless servant.'

I realised I had dropped my knees wide apart. Miranda was staring at my exposed cunt. My mouth was dry. I was overwhelmed by her story. My hands were shaking. I started to say something but I couldn't form my words properly.

'Drinks?'

It was Mandy.

Miranda asked for red wine. I nodded for the same – I didn't really know what I'd asked for.

Mandy opened my seat back table and placed the drinks onto it. Miranda reached over, and I took hold of her glass to pass it to her. I knocked it over. It broke and the shattered stem cut into the palm of her hand. The red wine spilled onto her wrist and knees. I grabbed her hand fussing and apologising profusely. I felt terrible! I drew her hand close to my face. I didn't know what I was doing. The blood was oozing from the wound – mixing with the dark red wine, dripping off the edge of her hand, dropping onto her wine soaked knees.

'I'm so sorry! So sorry! Here let me help! I'm so sorry.'

I pulled her hand closer to my face. I was staring at it. I couldn't take my eyes from it. The sight of the blood was captivating me – fixating me, drawing me to it.

'It's okay,' she said, her calm bearing obviously shaken.

'I'm so, so sorry! Here, let me kiss it. I can make it better.'

I don't know what I was thinking. It was the sight of the blood – her blood – and the flowing red wine, and her knees, wet and stained and apart, and the confusion, and the apology, and her graciousness, and her story still filling my head, and my trembling hands. It was everything! Everything drew me in, pulled me to the wound in her flesh, the seeping blood, the redness, the warmness of it. I cradled her hand – cupping it as if to drink. She didn't resist. I pulled it against my mouth, opened my lips and placed them against the cut. I tasted her blood – thick, luscious, velvety, profound. I sucked eagerly. I felt it flowing from the wound – being released by her body, allowing me to draw it up, to take it into myself. It was like breathing, like inhaling her very essence. I sucked harder. Yes, it was flowing freely; I was drinking from her, nourishing myself with her. Oh, the taste!

I looked up into her eyes. She was calm. She knew what I was doing. I sucked a little harder – increasing the flow, increasing the nourishment, increasing the pleasure, increasing my commitment.

'Oh dear! What has happened here?'

It was Mandy.

She fussed around attentively – offering tissues and busily trying to pick up the shattered pieces of glass. I wanted to tell her it was alright, that there was no need to bother, that we didn't need any help – to just go away! But, at the same time, I knew it was not appropriate to resist her help. It was enough for the moment. I had tasted blood again and knew that the desire for its flavour was still in me. I took my mouth from Miranda's wound. I knew her blood was smeared across my face, on my cheeks and nose – I could smell it, scent its delectable aroma.

Mandy pushed a tissue into my hand and tried to mop my face. I didn't know whether or not to let her or whether to do it myself.

I stood up to let Miranda past. I couldn't stop myself from running my hand between her buttocks as she squeezed by. She did not show approval or otherwise. I watched her go into the lavatory, hoping she would leave the door unlocked as an invitation for me to follow her, but when the "Occupied" sign came on I knew she had shut me out.

She did not say anything when she came back. She reached up into the overhead locker and moved things around before sitting down. She pulled a blanket over her knees and closed her eyes.

I pushed myself against her and listened to the deep hypnotic drone of the engines. All I could see in my mind was her cut hand. All I could taste in my mouth was her blood. All I could think about was drinking from her and wondering if it would ever happen again.

The next thing I knew the lights went on in the cabin. Passengers started to rouse themselves, put their jackets on, and get their bags down from the overhead lockers. The cabin staff brought out breakfast. I looked out of the window; the sun was rising – gold and red across the sea, colouring it red, like a massive ocean of blood.

Miranda pulled down the window blind.

Mandy offered Miranda a tray – coffee and croissants; not much. Mandy tapped a piece of folded note paper that was on the edge of the paper plate. Miranda nodded.

'What's that?' I asked wiping my bleary eyes.

'My next instruction. It doesn't stop you see, it never stops. It is my life now.'

She unfolded the note and read it slowly, nodding as she took it all in. I wanted to ask her what it said, who it was from, but I didn't dare. I hoped she would want to tell me, but she just put the note in her bag, took out her lipstick and pouted her full lips at its bright red point.

'I'll get your box down from the locker. It might be best to keep it under the seat for landing, don't you think? Where we can keep an eye on it?'

5. LONDON

The plane arrived late at London Heathrow. We circled the city for an hour before finally touching down at 1.30pm.

I walked out into the main building of Terminal Five with the plastic box hanging heavily from my hand. I felt tired from the flight. I went to the information desk and was directed to the "Connections" counter. The girl there – blonde with pale skin and a wide appealing mouth – told me there was not a direct connection to Bratislava. She looked at my note from Acme Couriers and passed it back to me with a shrug. The best she could do, she said, was a flight to Vienna and from there, she suggested, I take the train!

I couldn't believe it! I looked at the ticket wallet the man at Acme Couriers had pressed into my hand when I had left San Francisco. I had not looked in it since I had handed over my ticket in San Francisco. There was an envelope inside it. I opened it. On a note was written an address and the message: "Please make you own arrangements from London. This should cover it". Thirty ten dollar bills were pinned to the note. I swallowed hard. My first thought was to leave the box right there, in the middle of the terminal and just go. Then I thought I'd probably be arrested for abandoning a suspicious package, and then I realised that if I didn't get to the address with the box then I wouldn't get enough money to travel any further. And my fee for delivering the box would, I imagined, be more than three hundred dollars.

'Have you made up your mind?' asked the blonde haired girl behind the counter as she twisted her hair in a curl around her pencil. 'There are others waiting, you know.'

'Yes, of course. A single ticket to Vienna. Will this cover it?'

'I'm afraid there's only one flight a day to Vienna. And you've missed today's. The next flight is tomorrow at ten am, from this terminal. You've got a bit of a wait.' She held out my ticket and looked down the queue behind me. 'Next, please.'

I took the ticket and wandered off across the terminal. It was cavernous and overpowering. What was I going to do until ten o'clock the following morning? Everyone seemed to be going somewhere except me. I stared at some posters on a display board in front of a shop selling luggage. One in particular caught my eye: "Visit Hampton Court. Home of Henry VIII". 'Why not?' I thought. The palace of a king! That should occupy me for a few hours at least.

I struggled with the box to the taxi rank. It seemed to be weighing me down – it was as if it was getting heavier every time I picked it up!

'How much to Hampton Court?'

'That'll be thirty five pounds to you, dearie.'

'How much in dollars?'

'Now, let me see. Yes, seventy dollars would just about do it.'

I looked at my cash – not enough.

'Sorry, I'm a bit short. Sorry. I'll take a bus.'

'How much short?'

'Well, to be honest, I can only afford about ten dollars, well, nine actually.'

The driver got out and opened the rear door.

'What's in the box, dearie?'

'I don't know. What it says, I suppose.'

I held it up to show him.

'Wow! "HUMAN ORGAN"! I think you definitely need a lift. Hampton Court was it?'

'But I haven't got enough money.'

'Don't worry about that, dearie. I'm sure we can come to some arrangement. Don't you think?'

'Yes, I'm sure we can.'

I settled back into the sumptuous brown leather seat of the black taxi cab. I thought of how many others had sat here before me – how many bare bottoms had pressed against the shiny surface, how many cunts had squirmed down and moistened its ribbed corrugations.

He couldn't take his eyes off my knees. I tapped them with my hands, as though I was thinking of a tune in my head. I ran one of my fingers between them – just enough to open them so that the tip could slip in. My skin felt soft and smooth. I ran my fingertip around the insides of my knees – the light contact made me shiver.

I watched his eyes in the driving mirror – fixed entirely on what I was doing as I ran my fingertips up between my thighs. My skirt was short and barely covered my cunt. I took my finger up to its hem. He adjusted the mirror so that he could see more clearly. I lifted the hem slightly – just enough to show him the slit of my cunt. I opened my knees a little to ensure he had a good view of its narrow glistening crack.

The taxi slowed down in traffic then stopped. We were in a busy shopping street – held up by road works. People walked past – some shopping, some going to or coming from work, some sightseeing. A man peered into the taxi. I didn't stop what I was doing. The driver leant over the back of the seat and peered. He didn't say anything – just stared, wide eyed and engrossed.

Someone knocked on the window. A muffled voice shouted to the driver.

'I need to get to Kingston. Would your fare like to go halves?'

The driver wound down the window.

'Yes, mate. I think she might,' he said still not taking his eyes off me

The man peered in. I didn't even think of stopping. I opened my knees wider, exposing my cunt fully to him. I ran my finger along the wet slit – it was smooth and silky; the touch of its wetness sent a thrill through my hands and wrists. I tightened my buttocks as another surge of pleasure rose up between my thighs and this time penetrated my anus. As soon as I felt it, I opened my legs wider – I had no choice. I licked my lips then bit onto them. I felt the sharp ends of my canine teeth pressing down against their soft flesh.

The man opened the door and got in beside me. He was dressed in a dark business suit. He put his briefcase down in front of us, next to my plastic box. My heart was pounding. It was so exciting – being watched by the driver, and now a stranger, and not knowing what was going to happen next.

The man in the suit adjusted his tie – easing the strain of the tight collar around his neck. My hand was still between my legs. I drew it away, suddenly embarrassed by a realisation of my situation. My fingers were wet and glistened in a shaft of sunlight that came in through the taxi window.

'What have you been doing then?' asked the man.

I looked down and felt my cheeks burning.

'Enjoying yourself, by the look of it.'

I folded my arms and hid my wet hand from view.

'Though it's a bit naughty displaying yourself like this, in a taxi, so that anyone can see you. Don't you think? A bit naughty? Putting yourself on show so that anyone can see you – what you're doing?'

I didn't know what to say.

'A bit,' I muttered, still feeling desperately embarrassed.

'Yes, quite. Letting the taxi driver leer at you – see you – and then letting me do the same. Naughty, don't you think?'

'I suppose,' I said. 'Yes, I suppose.'

'I think some punishment is needed. Perhaps not too much, but enough to remind you that this sort of behaviour is inappropriate.'

His admonishment was so straightforward. He had only just got into the taxi, I didn't know who he was. He had no reason to take me to task and certainly no reason to think he could punish me, but still it seemed right somehow. I wanted him to tell me how he wanted to position me, what he wanted to do to me. I wanted to find out how much punishment he thought I should have, how much I would be allowed to scream out, how much of my pain he would allow me to release. I looked at him and bit my lips hard.

'Exactly,' he said. 'Here, bend over my knee. The best thing for you, I believe, is a sound spanking.'

My heart leapt at the thought. A spanking from a stranger, in a taxi travelling through the streets filled with people all of whom could look inside at any time and see what was happening to me.

I bent over his knees without any further question. He lifted my skirt. Straightaway I could tell he was annoyed. It was the way he sighed and tensed, I think – but it was obvious he was angry. I think it was because I had no panties on. Perhaps he thought it was shameless or immodest – I don't know.

He lifted my hips so that my bottom was raised. He told me to let my arms and head hang down freely. He said I could rest my hands on the floor. If I squirmed, he said, I would receive more, and they would be harder as well.

He started straightaway – a sudden hard smack. It stung terribly. I gasped. It was really hard. He smacked me again – this time even harder. My eyes widened and I gasped again. Another hard smack followed, and another. I couldn't keep still. I reached my hands back, stupidly trying to stop him, stupidly trying to prevent him from carrying out my punishment. He knocked my hands away and smacked me even harder for trying to prevent him. From then on it was relentless – smack followed smack, stinging pain followed stinging pain. I squirmed and fought against him, but nothing stopped him. I couldn't stand it – it was too much, too sudden, too painful, too deliberate – but he wouldn't stop.

I threw my head back, still trying to avoid his blows, but he was too strong and held me too firmly across his knees. I saw figures outside the taxi – faces staring in. People were looking at what was going on – ogling me, seeing my bottom tipped over my punisher's knees, watching his spanking hand thrashing me so hard, seeing the cheeks of my buttocks reddened and smudged with the bruising he was inflicting on me.

I know I was shouting for him to stop – screaming I think – but it only ended when he decided it would, and that was longer than I could ever have imagined.

I felt the taxi stop, I saw more faces at the window. I felt myself being pushed from his knees onto the floor. For a few seconds I lay at his feet – depleted and racked with pain and humiliation. I struggled onto the seat. I couldn't sit down, my bottom was too sore.

A wad of money dropped by the side of me.

'That should cover my half of the fare I think.'

As he left and closed the door behind him, I counted the money. It was £200!

Hampton Court was beautiful – the sun shone on its mellow, red bricked turrets, the golden crosses on their tops glistened and twinkled like stars, its massive chimneys heaved up into the sky like the cores of long eroded volcanoes. Opening times were ten until six – I could spend the whole day here! I waited at the gate while the handsome young guide for a group of giggling Japanese girls discussed the entrance fees. The distraction was sufficient for me to push in behind them without being seen. My nine dollars was still intact, and so was my £200!

I walked beneath the high beamed roof of the medieval Great Hall. A guard pushed me back when I touched one of the huge tapestries which hung from the walls – endless depictions of hunting scenes and amorous lovers cradled in each other's arms. Their stale linen scent stuck to my fingers.

The Japanese group came in noisily, flashing their cameras and chattering excitedly amongst themselves. The guide – a handsome young man – held a Japanese flag on a stick. Whenever he called out to his charges he waved the stick and they all gathered around him like cheeping chickens. They all wore short red and black tartan skirts, loose leather belts, white shirts and red scarves pulled into toggles at their necks. Two in particular caught my eye – a little different from the rest. They held onto each other's arms – one with red spiky hair, the other with black hair spiked in the same way, black lipstick and a silver ring in her nose. These two had black leather boots loosely crumpled around their ankles and white socks that were pulled up to just below their knees. Both of them smiled demurely at me before each pointing their toes together and looking down to the ground with slightly flushed cheeks. Some of the others giggled at them. They were entrancing. I was captivated by them and couldn't stop myself from following them.

For a while they walked arm in arm alongside the rest of the group but, touching the surfaces of tables with their fingers, or stopping to look at painting hung on the walls, they slowly drifted apart from the others. In the end, they separated themselves completely. Checking that no one could see them, they stepped into a narrow entrance leading off the main room. I hung back until I knew they had gone in far enough so that I would be able to follow them without them seeing me.

When I thought it was safe, I followed them into the darkness. It smelled musty and damp. As my eyes slowly became used to the darkness, I saw several full sized statues lined up along one side of a narrow corridor. I stood in front of one – a knight in armour with a sword hanging at an angle from a scabbard at his belt. They looked creepy – all that attention, unmoving, heavy and stiff. Ahead, I could see the two girls giggling and chattering. The sound of their excited voices echoed against the heavy stonework of the walls. I saw their profiles silhouetted against the light ahead – slim shadowy creatures, their spiky hair sticking out at random angles from their heads like sharp, stiff fingers.

They clutched each other's cheeks in their hands and kissed. I watched them pulling their small cherub-like mouths close, locking their eager lips, pressing their small firm breasts against each other, rising up pleasurably in each other's keen embrace. The one with the red hair, I think, ran her hand up the other's thigh – lifting her short skirt, revealing her tight white panties, running her fingers across the taut material that clung closely to her springy bottom. The revealed curve of her buttocks was delightful – a smooth arc running from the tops of her thighs and leading up naturally to her narrow belted waist. The light pleated material of her tartan skirt lifted easily and fell against her smooth skin in soft lazy folds. The red haired girl's hand floated across the delightful arc – hardly glancing the skin, just caressing its peach-like surface with only the lightest touch.

I pressed myself against the cold stone wall and brought my fingers up between my legs. I gasped with relief as my fingers entered my warm wet cunt. Spit ran over my bottom lip as if in recognition of this immediate fulfilment.

I listened to their amorous groans, their slurping hungry lips, the ardent pressure of their bodies one against the other. Each new sound made me force my fingers deeper – each groan, each slurp, each rubbing sound feeding my own hunger for more, my own need for pleasure and ultimate satisfaction.

I realised I was groaning as well, slurping, pressing my body noisily against the wall. Suddenly I thought that they might hear me! I went still – frozen, my fingers pressed deeply into my slit, spit running from my mouth and dripping down my chin. I listened to my heart pounding – my blood pulsating through my veins, thumping in my temples, making me giddy and hot. I backed away, frightened that they might see me and stop, terrified that they might leave me like this – bound with unreleased joy, confined by my anticipation, seized with a desperate need for fulfilment. I felt the statue behind me – hard and cold. I felt the hilt of the sword pressing against my buttocks – thick and stiff.

The two girls pulled away from each other – standing back and holding hands, bowing their heads, licking their lips, recovering for a moment from the heat of their passion. I wanted to run up to them and kiss them one by one. I wanted to lift their skirts, to run my hands across their bottoms, to slip my fingers between their legs and feel the soft flesh of their cunts pulled tightly against the thin white material of their panties. I wanted to strip their clothes off in a madness of passion – throw them both to the ground naked, spread their legs and lick their delectable slits as they wriggled and squealed beneath me.

I pressed myself back more against the statue – hiding away from the girls, fearful of discovery, fearful of the uncontrolled release of my own passions.

They swung their hands between them, rocking from side to side as if playing a school yard game. They dropped their heads sideways in rhythm with their movements. I found myself moving in time with them – pushing back, leaning forward before pushing back again at the same pace as their slowly swinging arms.

Suddenly, I heard footsteps. Someone was coming!

The girls kept swinging their hands – side to side, rocking their heads, smiling at each other silently.

A man appeared from beyond them. I could only see his silhouette – tall, slim, with loose clothing. He stopped as if startled or surprised by seeing the two girls in front of him. They giggled but continued swinging their hands. He approached them and spoke. I couldn't hear what he said nor could I hear their reply.

I pressed back against the statue. I felt the rounded pommel at the end of the handle against the parting cheeks of my buttocks. I bent forward enough to widen the gap between them. The pommel felt heavy and massive. I lifted myself slightly against it.

The two girls each released one of their hands. They turned sideways to face the man. They ducked a little, still chatting and giggling. One of them pawed at him with her free hand, the other followed her partner's lead. They stroked his face and ran their hands around his neck and along his shoulders. I could see he was flattered by their attention. He reached out to them but they pulled back, still with their single hands entwined and giggled loudly as though avoiding him was some sort of victory, like winning a race or game.

Suddenly he caught hold of one of them – perhaps the one with the red hair, I wasn't sure. He held her by the arm and drew her close to his chest. She struggled but could not free herself. She whinnied like a captured fawn. Her friend pulled at her hand, trying to release her from the man's grasp, but he held on too strongly and would not let her go.

I was transfixed. I realised I was rubbing the pommel of the sword handle between my buttocks now. I had leant forward and opened them wide enough for the cold round carved pommel to press against my anus. Its hardness felt brutal and unyielding, its rough surface abrasive and dry. I pressed harder and felt its force on the edge of my exposed anal ring. I gasped and felt my heart beating wildly in my chest. I pushed my fingers deeper into my cunt then pulled them out and ran my wet hand between my legs and rubbed it onto the stone sword pommel. I stroked my wet hand around it, feeling its girth, its strength its hardness. I lubricated it with my own moisture then plunged my fingers back into my cunt and pressed my anus harder against the now-wet pommel.

The man twisted the girl's arm behind her back and pulled her tightly against him. He pressed his mouth against hers. She struggled and tried to escape but he wouldn't let her go and twisted her arm to bring her under control. Her friend punched at the man but he was too strong and her blows fell meaninglessly onto his well muscled body. He pushed the red haired girl to her knees. Her friend stood back. He gave some instructions and the girl on her knees reached up and undid the front of his trousers. The black haired girl dropped to her knees by her friend's side.

I watched the red haired girl draw out the man's cock – it was big and hard. I imagined its heat, its firmness its pulsating, vein covered shaft. I pressed myself more fully against the pommel and allowed my anus to open under the increased pressure. I gasped as I felt the wet-smeared, stone knob touching the delicate inside of my anus. For a moment I held my breath, wondering if I dare press more – wondering if my delicate flesh could take the size, the hardness, the roughness.

I watched the red haired girl's mouth open. Her lower jaw dropped wide as she fed the swollen end of the cock between her lips. She rose up on it, as if she was inhaling it. Her dark haired companion waited by her side, still holding her friend's hand but no longer trying to help her escape or free herself. Now they were both under a different sort of control – it was not physical although it manifested itself in a physical way, it was purely spirit that exerted itself completely over everything material. They were under a strange and powerful spell, operating now under the magic of some force more dominant than anything connected to the physical world.

I watched the red haired girl's cheeks dish in as she sucked hard on the massive cock. I pressed myself harder against the pommel. It entered my anus, first expanding it, pressuring its edges, then springing inside; released by the tension at the entrance and straightaway revelling in the comparative ease to be found inside my rectum. I drew in breath with a noisy gasp. I held it in, fearful that I had been heard and would be detected. When I tried to breathe out I couldn't release it and waited, blocked by it, my lungs exploding, as only gradually it seeped away.

The red haired girl's head moved up and down on the heavy shaft in her mouth – her spiky hair bending back and forth, her slim frame submitting itself to the spell of the beating blood-filled hardness inside her mouth. I knew she was licking it with her tongue, wrapping it eagerly around its end, licking around the sensitive rear edge of the glans, feeling the texture of the raised pulsating veins as she allowed it to go deeper towards the back of her throat.

I saw it enter as far as it could, then I saw her hold it at its limit. I knew the swollen glans was pressed against the back of her throat then, as she gulped and pressed further, I knew she had yielded to it and taken it further down. I knew it was going down her throat then, as she pressed her gaping lips hard against the base of his stomach, I knew it was fully in. She kept it there, holding it in place, allowing the lining of her throat to tighten against it, binding itself to her as if it was part of her.

I rode the pommel in my rectum. I plunged my fingers deeper into my cunt. I wanted the cock the red haired girl was sucking in my mouth. I so wanted to take it down my throat, to feel its throbbing end as deep as it would go. Spit ran from my mouth as the rough harness of the pommel went deeper and I felt the following hardness of the thick ribbed handle which it topped.

Suddenly the cock exploded from the girl's mouth. There was so much of it! She choked and coughed. Immediately, her waiting friend grasped it and took it into her mouth. She sucked hard and without hesitation or delay took it down straightaway. She threw her hands up in the air, pinioned by the full length of the heavy cock deep inside her throat. Her friend held onto her, encouraging her to keep it in longer, to take it even deeper, to nourish herself completely.

I didn't know what I was doing anymore. I felt completely filled – stuffed full of the hard rough handle of the sword. I didn't know how much was inside me, how much I could take, how much more I was going to take. I thrust my other hand down and pressed hard around the base of my clitoris. The tops of my thighs were soaking wet with the moisture flowing from my cunt.

The man's cock came out of the dark haired girls' throat. Like her friend she choked and coughed. Spit sprayed from her mouth. They held onto each other, kissing, tasting the man's cock on their lips, sucking in each other's spit, trying to satisfy themselves. But they were not satisfied – I could see that. They got up from their knees and draped themselves around the man's neck. He bent his face to them and they reached their faces up to his. They kissed him for a few moments then the girl with the red hair pressed her mouth against one side of his neck. Her friend did the same on the other side. The man allowed his head to fall back in an ecstasy as they kissed his neck, then I heard him cry out in pain and shock as they both bit deeply into this flesh.

I tightened on the hard shaft in my anus – I was surprised and shocked – and, as I did, I felt a seizure of pleasure running deep inside my hips, into my stomach, and up into my chest. I gasped and started panting loudly. I didn't care anymore if I was heard or detected. I pressed back harder and felt the pommel deep inside my rectum – I was filled with it, stuffed completely. I felt as if I was hanging on it, like a flag on a staff – weak and exhausted, pinioned by it, penetrated by it, no longer able to remain in control of myself.

I watched the two girls biting into the man's neck. They did not just make punctures big enough to drink from, they bit again and again, lacerating his skin, breaking it open and covering the surface with bloody wounds. They were like wild dogs feeding frantically on their prey. They took no notice of his cries, they ignored his screams; I could not tell whether they were screams of pain or cries for mercy – it did not matter. I watched the silhouetted blood spurting from his throat. I watched the two ravenous figures lapping at the wounds, chasing the torrents of blood that ran down their victim's neck. I watched the girls writhing in the stream, bathing in the falling tide of blood, eating the flesh of their prey, taking at last what had always been their need, saturating themselves in the crimson fluid they so much craved.

Weakened, the man fell back against the wall – his head drooped, his arms loosely by his side. Still they fed on him, laughing, giggling, biting, making fresh wounds, fresh punctures from which his precious blood could run. They stopped occasionally and kissed each other, lapping at the blood on each other's faces, or passing it between their mouths with their bubbling spit.

I hung on the solid sword handle, depleted and worn out. I was twitching – I knew my passion had flowed, that my orgasm had overwhelmed me, but I couldn't remember it. My body felt tense and cramped and yet I was wilted and limp. I was gasping, panting, my cunt was aching, my rectum still felt stuffed and my anus was painful and sore. I didn't think I would be able to move again. I was completely overwhelmed.

For a moment my eyes were closed. I imagined the seizure that must have overtaken me – the lights in my head, the aching in my rectum, the uncontrollable spasms throughout my convulsing body. When I opened them again the girls were standing in front of me, holding hands, giggling, staring at me inquisitively. They were soaked – their shirts and socks were red, their faces covered and dripping with blood, their knees smudged with the man's ruby nectar. They smiled at me. It was as if nothing had happened. They giggled. The one with the red hair pawed at my face.

'Pretty,' she said, and they both giggled. 'Very pretty.'

They both smiled broadly. Their sharp canine teeth glistened. I dropped my head to the side, exposing my neck to them, hoping they would fall on me and devour me in the same way they had taken the man. I looked into their eyes appealing for their attention but they just giggled again and ran off down the dim corridor to join with their chattering, inquisitive party.

I went back to Heathrow and slept in the main terminal building. It was fairly quiet for most of the night. I had a breakfast burger and salad in "Giraffe" and, with most of my money still intact, I was the first to board the plane to Vienna.

6. THE TRAIN TO BRATISLAVA

I thought Vienna would be surrounded by mountains – a panorama of snow capped peaks bathed in fresh air and flowers. I couldn't have been more wrong – it was flat, dirty and grimy. The backstreets were tawdry, the bars sleazy and architecture too big and grandiose to deal with. There were fountains everywhere – massive stampeding horses ridden by naked windblown gods, muscular warriors fighting serpents, cherubs and angels with trumpets striving for the right to challenge or serve a greater god.

The bus from the airport stopped at the front entrance to Vienna Reichsbrücke station – a maze of tramlines, yellow road markings, and zigzagging taxis weaving between people with every size and description of bag it is possible to imagine.

I bought a ticket to Bratislava and soon found the right platform. I looked up at the chattering information board – an hour to wait and an hour to get there. I sat on a wooden bench and stared at the clock – it seemed stuck on one o'clock. I pushed the plastic box between my feet and looked around. A young woman stood in front of me facing the rails. She wore a pink dress with a short skirt and a deeply cut neckline. She placed her red leather bag on the ground and bent one foot around the top of her other ankle. She dropped her hips sideways and balanced herself with perfect poise. She had a beautiful figure – tall, slender, strikingly curved with square shoulders.

It was an old fashioned train; the passenger coaches separated into compartments each seating eight people. It was very hot – the middle of summer and the heating was switched on! A girl opposite me took out a frilly white handkerchief and mopped her pale forehead. She pressed it to her lips and seemed refreshed by her own salty wetness. A man sitting near the window wiped his face with the back of his hand. I imagined him offering it to the young woman to lick. I pictured her stroking her tongue across its surface, taking up the salt – the salt that had been squeezed from the pores of his flesh by the heat that had built up inside him. The thought sent a shivering thrill down between my hips. Just before the last train door slammed shut, the woman in the pink dress who had stood in front of me on the platform sat down by my side.

The train pulled out noisily – heavy diesel engine noise, lots of clatter over uneven rail points, loud clanking and sudden snagging of ungreased and ill maintained rolling stock couplings.

Everybody had only just settled – opening their books, a magazine, eating a cream cake – when the compartment door was pushed open. It made me jump. Two men in dark blue uniforms pushed their way in. Both of them wore shiny peaked caps and carried handguns in holsters fixed to black leather belts pulled tightly around their waists. Neither had shaved for several days. One had a blue tattoo of an eagle on the back of his hand.

' Pasů!' he announced. 'Passports!'

Everyone started to search in their bags and pockets.

He kicked at the box at my feet.

'Co je v krabici? Co je krabici?'

'Sorry. I don't understand?'

'Co je krabici!'

'Sorry, I – '

'Krabici! Krabici!'

I held out my passport. It only angered him.

'Krabici! Krabici!'

The woman in the pink dress pressed her mouth against my ear – her breath was cool and refreshing, as though she was breathing out the fragrance of a high mountain stream. I felt my lips going dry.

'What's in the box?' she whispered. 'They want to know what's in your box.'

I picked up the box and held it in front of them.

'Hu...man or...gan,' I said slowly and loudly. 'Hu...man or...gan.'

The woman laughed.

'I don't think that will help too much. Shampoo and makeup would be better, I think,' she said quietly. She looked up at the nearest man. 'Шампунь и состав.' He shrugged dismissively. She turned back to me 'They're Russian anyway. Don't speak a word of English! And their Czech's not so good either! Left over after the Cold War ended with nowhere to go, I suppose. Take any job as long as it's got a uniform – you know the type.'

The official weighed the box in his hand and nodded knowingly. He put it back down on the floor between my feet and asked the woman for her passport.

'Can we come to an arrangement? Можем мы приходим к расположению?' she said opening her red leather bag.

The official bent down to it and removed a bottle of vodka. She turned again to me.

'In this country, you can get anything for the right price.'

She presented her passport to him. He opened the first page and frowned. There was a loose picture in the front with something written on it. He twisted it sideways and read the note. He looked at her enquiringly then back at the note. He rubbed his stubbly chin, smiled then nodded.

'Anything,' she said in my ear. 'You can get anything for the right price in Slovakia.'

Another thrill passed through me as again her fresh mountain breath wafted into my nostrils.

She followed the first unformed official out of the compartment and, as if being escorted, she walked between both of them down the corridor.

I pushed the box underneath the seat. It felt warm. I imagined it must be well insulated.

I stared through the window. We travelled past flat, bleak areas of brown and green rolling countryside. I saw a white light on the horizon and couldn't work out what it was. As we got closer I realised it was a mass of buildings – a massive estate of regulation height white blocks of flats, leftovers from a previous political era, testament to a now-lost time of purpose and commitment. After a while another one appeared and then another – all the same, indistinguishable, glistening prisons for their captured inhabitants.

I felt bored and began to wonder where the woman in the pink dress had gone with the uniformed customs men. I left the compartment and wandered down the corridor looking for her.

Passengers were keen to get out of the hot compartments and lined the corridors. Men laughed and joked with young women, smokers hung out of windows, dogs sat obediently outside compartments. I squeezed past them all, sometimes facing them, sometimes turning away. I walked almost the full length of the train until I came to the guard's van. The train went into a tunnel and for a few minutes I was in complete darkness. When we emerged with a loud clatter onto a steel lattice work bridge the brightness was so sudden I couldn't see anything clearly.

As my eyes got used to the flickering light I began to make out what was in front of me. There was a steel mesh cage around a partitioned off area. Tattered parcels and torn postal bags lay around untidily in one corner. At the other end, barely visible in the flashing light and darkness, I could just about make out a figure. I could hear some voices but couldn't see who they belonged to and couldn't make out what was being said.

Suddenly, the train was over the bridge and in full sunlight. The flashing stopped, everything came into focus. The figure was the young woman in the pink dress – the one who had left with the customs officials! She was hanging from a heavy hook in the roof of the carriage, her full weight slumped on her wrists which were bound together tightly by a rope lashed around the hook. Her right hip was dropped to the side, her toes, hardly touched the ground. One of her red shoes had fallen off and was lying on its side. Slightly to her side were the two men, their peaked caps shining in the shards of light that flashed through small windows in the top edges of the carriage roof. They both looked up and down her captive body – muttering, laughing, conspiring.

She stared ahead silently – waiting for something to happen to her that was out of her control, knowing that her fate was being planned by others, that her destiny was still to be revealed.

Her dress fitted her so closely – following the curve of her hips, the line of her waist and firm mounds of her breasts as if it was a second skin. Her mouth was slightly open, her full lips – glossy and luscious – moved in a slow shiver as if she was saying a prayer or reciting the supplicant's part in a catechism. Her dress was so thin that I could see she was not wearing any bra or panties.

One of the men shouted something at the captive woman. She responded slowly and in a low mutter. Annoyed, he shouted again, this time louder and with more aggression. She started again, making an effort but still not to his satisfaction. He snapped at her angrily. She spoke up this time, obeying his insistence, staring ahead, not looking him in the eye, speaking as clearly as she could so that there was no misunderstanding. It seemed to satisfy him. He nodded to the other man who nodded back.

I crouched against the edge of the wire barrier that contained them. The echoing clatter of the rail tracks filled my ears. The shafts of sunlight flashing through the small windows in the roof dazzled me. I was hypnotised by it all – overcome by the sensation of rhythmic noise and blinking light, enthralled by the predicament of the captive woman, filled with anxiety brought on by my spying. I hung onto the edge of the steel framework that supported the large wire enclosure, pressing my face against it, feeling its coolness and the roughness of the small rivets that ran along it edges, kissing the raised points where the wires of the mesh crossed over one another.

The man said something else to the woman. She replied again, this time insistently as if she was arguing against him. He spoke again and again she raised her voice to him. He squeezed his hand on either side of her cheeks – forcing her luscious lips into a pout – and brought his face close to hers. He shook her head from side to side. He released her suddenly and she shouted again, this time spitting at him.

He turned away from her angrily, striding about, taking deep breaths, screwing up his lips and frowning heavily. Her spit dribbled down his cheek and the side of his nose. My heart was beating fast. I was fearful for the woman yet excited by her treatment. I was trapped – my fear for her predicament fed my excitement of what was happening to her, and of what might happen to her. My mind filled with the possibilities; they boiled over inside me in a turmoil of confusion, fear, and excitement.

The pacing man suddenly turned and wrapped his arms around the woman's hips. He lifted her off the ground. The other man dragged over a large wooden box. He stood on it, reached up and shortened the ropes that bound her wrists and led up to the hook in the roof to which they were attached. He yanked on the rope until it was tight again. The first man then let the woman go and she fell heavily onto the rope. She yelled out as the rope snatched tight. Her body hung well clear of the ground – her head dropped forward, her arms pulled up tightly, her feet twitched and crossed over each other, her toes stretched out in a vain attempt to find the ground.

I pressed myself tighter against the wire mesh, harder against the rivets, harder against the raised connections in the intertwined wire. Seeing the weight of the woman's body hanging on the rope, the stretched tautness of her arms, her powerlessness, combined inside me in shivers of fear. I imagined being in her place – feeling the pressure on my wrists, knowing what it was like to be another's victim, feeling the power of another overwhelming me. I thought of myself as their victim – abject, humiliated, waiting only to be the subject of their wishes. That sense of subjection to the will of another was the greatest thrill. Of all the sensations that were filling me, this was the most arousing. I licked at the wire mesh, tasting its metallic tang and the thrill of its sharp flavour sent a wave of shivering delight that penetrated me from my toes and ankles into my neck and face. I felt the hardness of the wire against my teeth as I opened my mouth against it – licking at it, savouring it, luxuriating in its inanimate lifelessness.

The man who had lifted the woman went to a bag on the floor and took something from it – a ball gag with a broad leather strap. He held it on front of the woman's face and shouted at her. I think he was remonstrating with her for talking, or for talking too much or too loudly – it didn't seem to matter. She shook her head, perhaps saying she did not mean what she had said, or did not mean to seem disobedient, or resentful, or contrary. He shouted louder – her defence only seemed to anger him more. Again she shook her head but I could tell that now she knew her efforts had been pointless, that it had only increased his anger and would only increase the vengeful way that he punished her. Yes, I could see in her eyes – still staring ahead but now vacuous and hopeless – that she knew she should not have answered back, should not have believed it worthwhile defending herself. Yes, now I could see that she knew that what would follow would only be worse because of her stupidity. At the same time I could see in her face that she knew in truth that no effort on her part would have altered her destiny – it had been sealed from the beginning.

I licked the crossed wires of the mesh, feeling my spit running onto them, flowing onto the intersecting points of metal wire, cooling and spreading across their surface before I licked it back and sucked at it like some delectable nectar. I ran my tongue into the joints until it pinched between them and was held fast when I tried to tug it back.

The man pulled the woman's jaw down and held her mouth open – wide, exposing, empty. He pressed the ball gag against her stretched lips – it was too big to enter her mouth. I watched him press it hard against her teeth for a second or two. Still it refused to go in, then as he lifted his elbow and brought more strength to bear, it suddenly sprang inside, fixed behind her teeth, and stuffed her mouth completely.

Her mouth was strained so wide. I opened my own mouth – unthinkingly at first – mimicking her, seeing if I could do the same. When I realised I couldn't, a shiver of fear went through me at the thought that her mouth was stretched so much and plugged so fully. I couldn't imagine how the ball could come out again. I opened my mouth again, and felt the tingling of tightness in the corners of my lips, but still I knew it was not open enough to take the massive ball that was now firmly locked inside the woman's mouth.

The man tightened the leather strap behind her head. Her eyes were wide open, filled with terror. Her nostrils flared open as she sucked in air, desperate to inhale, terror stricken by the huge plug in her mouth and now by its fixing with the strap. She looked so trapped and fearful. I could see the depths of her fear in the wideness of her beautiful eyes and the openness of her dilated nostrils. I could see her terror in the limpness of her body and the inescapable proneness to another captured in her powerless stretched out arms.

The other man spun her around. She whirled on the rope at her wrists, her eyes even wider as she fought to stop herself succumbing to dizziness. The rope tightened and curled up in a tight knot. It bound up around itself and pinched into the skin of her wrists. I could see she wanted to scream. Each time her face flashed in front of me, each time the image of her terror was caught in the erratic light from the windows in the carriage, I imagined her screeching cries as syncopations to the frantic clattering of the steel wheels on the tracks beneath our feet. Each time she spun around, the sound of her unheard yells kept pace with the pounding of my wildly beating heart.

Her spinning stopped when the rope bound up in such a tight knot it would wind no further. For a moment she remained hanging there – silent, motionless, experiencing a moment of peace. Then, slowly at first, the rope began to unwind itself. Quickly her spinning gathered pace and, as both men helped rotate her faster by pushing at her, she eventually found herself hanging on the rope that was bound tight onto itself at the other extreme. Again, a pause, a few seconds of peace before the terrible torture began again.

They stood back and watched her as she spun in decreasing revolutions first one way and then the next until, in the end, she remained still – hanging motionless on the rope. I could see from her eyes that she was giddy – her pupils wandered sideways, unable to fix on anything, unable to focus properly on a firm and dependable part of the world. I thought how she must be thinking of vomiting, worrying that her throat would be filled with it, that she would not be able to allow it out and that she would need to choke and cough but even that would be impossible. I imagined her panic and felt some of it myself.

One of the men took something else from the bag. It was a heavy leather strap, about the length of his arm, as wide as three fingers and finished at one end into a rounded handle. He turned it through a wide arc. The flashing light through the roof windows of the carriage picked it up like a strobe. The highlighted strap seemed to move through the air in distinct phases, changing position without being seen and reappearing in the next position as if out of thin air. He smacked it down on his hand. It was heavy and loud. The woman stared at it – following its flight through the air, fixing on its sound when it slapped his hand. Even though it was impossible for her to show it, I knew her fear was increasing with every curving sweep and every smacking crack. Yes, if it was imaginable, her panic was being redoubled by every threat that was being put before her.

I pushed my fingers through the wire mesh, folding them around it, clawing onto it like a prisoner hoping for escape. But I didn't want to escape, I wanted to see it all, I wanted to hear it all, sense it all, experience it all.

The clattering of the train wheels filled my head. The flashing of the sunlight through the roof windows blurred my vision. The fear in the woman's eyes sent my blood pounding around my veins. I pressed myself against the corner of the wire mesh cage. I opened my legs and pressed the slit of my cunt against the sharp metal edge. I moved up and down against it, rubbing my soft flesh against the rivets that held the mesh to the frame. They caught against my clitoris – pulling at it painfully and filling me with wave after wave of delectable, cutting joy. I licked the mesh and spread my spit across it, imagining it running down to my crack, lubricating it and allowing it to slide even more easily against the hard angled rivet studded metal of the frame.

There was a sudden crack. For a moment I didn't know if it was the wheels of the train crashing over some uneven points, or the blasting increase of air pressure as the train entered a tunnel. I soon realised it was neither. It was the heavy leather strap being brought across the woman's bottom. The men had lifted up the hem of her dress and twisted it around the waist of her dress. I hadn't even seen them doing it – I had been so engaged with myself. Her bottom was bare, she had no panties on. It was a beautiful shape – a delightful smooth curve, a satiny surface of perfectly smooth skin slightly moistened by tiny beads of sweat. And the hard leather of the strap had already left its mark.

It came down again. This time I followed it as it flashed from place to place in the flickering light from the windows in the carriage roof. Each of its positions was frozen, each of its positions was a surprise. Then, when it made contact with her taut skin, it seemed to hang there longer than anywhere else; as if it were allowing the pain to soak in deeper and longer. The woman flinched when it struck, she twisted away from it but she had nothing to purchase on. All she could do was spin randomly, twist sometimes in a way that allowed the blow to be lessened, sometimes in a way that only made it worse.

Every time the sunlight flashed across her body I saw the red lines left by the heavy leather strap. To start with they were isolated – easy to distinguish and clear edged. After a while they were impossible to distinguish one from another. Like tracks across a crimson desert, they all smudged together into one angry red mass laced with purple stripes. I could see the strap was hard edged and every blow brought its hard edges down sharply against the woman's skin. There was nothing to save her from the punishment, nothing to save her from the power of the strap or the cutting of its inflexible edges.

I hadn't known how much I had pressed my crack against the edge of the metal framework. I only realised when I felt the pain. I pulled back and dropped my head. I dribbled my spit down onto my slit as I listened to the punishment the woman was having, all the time imagining the cries she would make if she was able. I watched my spit running into my crack – glistening in the flashing light that came in through the windows in the carriage roof. I was hypnotised by it all – transported.

I don't know when it all finished. I know I jerked against the metal frame as I was overcome with a shuddering ecstasy. I know that it hurt and that made the ecstasy continue. I know I licked the mesh as I watched the redness of the woman's bottom increase with every savage blow. I know I imagined myself screaming in her place, and was not sure that I did not. In the end it was the strange echoing return to the clattering sound of the wheels on the tracks that brought me around. And as I listened to it I finally realised there was nothing else to come – the punishment had ended.

I looked up and watched the woman. She swung from side to side, twisting slowly, completely used and utterly used up. She had no further pain to give, no more suffering left. It was all inside her, none of it had escaped, it had all been contained by the plug in her mouth. She had not given a single cry of pain, a single whimper. She had not begged for them to stop, or screamed out for mercy. She had not blubbered words that could not be understood because she was too confused and too terrified. She had not let any of it go.

The one who had flogged her held her around the waist while the other man undid the rope at her wrists. They let her drop to the floor. She tried to curl up and hold her knees but the pain obviously prevented her. They pulled her dress down over her exposed cunt then tried to get the ball gag out of her mouth. It was too tight. They had to hold her jaw wide and prise it from behind her teeth. After some effort it came out in an explosive blast. Behind it her mouth and throat were full of spit. It ran down her chin and neck and over the front of her dress in a glistening stream.

The two men stood back – one folding his arms, the other putting his hands in his pockets. They both seemed to be waiting for something.

I kept watching her as she rubbed her bottom and winced, as she coughed and wiped the spit from her mouth and chin. Suddenly she looked straight at me. She was not surprised or ashamed. I could see that it was obvious she had known I was there all the while. Yes, she had known all the time that I had been watching her, that I had seen her punishment, her pain and her terror.

Her penetrating stare confused me. I didn't understand what was going on. The two men took no notice.

She reached out her hand. She motioned towards something – her hand was limp and weak, she could hardly lift it. She was pointing to the red leather bag which lay, undone and on its side. I widened my eyes to see if that was what she was pointing to. She nodded shakily. I didn't know what to do.

'It's alright,' she said. 'It's alright, really.'

I looked at the men. They both looked down to the ground.

Hesitantly, I walked around the edge of the wire mesh enclosure and in through the flimsy door. I was shaking all over. The zip of the bag was undone. It was her bag. I recognised it now. I opened the top. There was a wad of money held together with a plastic band.

'Yes, yes,' she said weakly. 'Give them the money. Please. Give them the money. It's alright, I promise you.'

My hands were shaking as I dipped them into the bag. I took the money out and, still on my knees, held it out to the man nearest. He leered, took it from me, sat down on a large wooden chest with his comrade, took the elastic band off and began counting it.

'You see,' she continued in a hoarse whisper. 'You can get anything for the right price in Slovakia. Anything you want.'

I suddenly realised what was happening – she was paying them! She had paid them for her punishment and suffering! Anything could be had at the right price, she had said! This terrible punishment had been her need, and the price she had paid had been enough to satisfy it.

'Anything you want,' she said faintly as her eyes turned upwards and she dropped back to the ground unconscious.

The train stopped against the buffers in Bratislava station with a sudden heavy jolt. I leant out of the window of the guard's van door. People gathered their belongings together and sidled their way down the corridors. They spilled out onto the platform and scurried off in every direction. There was no uniform flow – it was as if every direction led to an exit. I was caught up in the frantic confusion of movement.

Suddenly, in a panic, I ran down the corridor to the compartment I had been sitting in. It was empty. I bent down to pick up the box. It had gone! I couldn't believe it! The box had gone!

I went hot. Sweat broke out on my forehead. My legs felt hollow. The box had gone! I had lost it! Someone had taken it! I spun around. I felt giddy. I looked for it on the seats, on the luggage racks, out of the window! It was nowhere to be seen. I darted out into the corridor and looked its full length each way. I ran from carriage to carriage, flinging open the WC doors, looking behind them, grabbing people, pulling at their luggage. But the box had gone! The box I had been entrusted with in San Francisco had gone!

My heart was beating madly. I was gasping for breath. I didn't know what to do! In a blind panic and filled with confusion, I jumped off the train. I was shaking all over.

I saw two young women running away near the exit. Their shiny clothing flashed in the sunlight that broke in through the gaps in the high station roof. They were carrying the box between them – laughing, jumping excitedly, running through the bustling throng of people as though they weren't there. They looked like elves on a mission for their lord.

I took a couple of paces in their direction. Straightaway I was stopped by a young man. He stood in front of me, holding out his hand, begging. I dodged him but he grabbed hold of my arm. I pushed him away but he pushed back and I fell on the ground. I sprawled on the dirty concrete platform, surrounded by the legs of the hurrying crowd, confused, desperate, filled with panic and struggling to get to my feet.

The man ran off. I looked for the two girls with the box but they had disappeared – like elfin spirits they had evaporated into the noise and movement of the bustling city.

I struggled onto my hands and knees, picking up the contents of my bag that had fallen out around me. I dragged my passport from underneath someone's foot. People were staring at me, pointing in disgust. I realised that my short skirt had ridden up around my waist and my naked bottom was fully exposed to their glare. My face was red with embarrassment as I pulled it down and got to my feet.

7. THE MEETING

Confused and shaking all over, I muddled my way to an exit and stepped out into the street. I felt dishevelled and bewildered. It was as hot as it had been on the train, very noisy and the streets were packed with cars, taxis, trams and people. The air was filled with the scent of coffee and cigarettes. I felt giddy and rested against a large tattered street map pasted on the wall of a news kiosk.

I couldn't believe what had happened. I had lost the box! I dropped my head and shook it from side to side in disbelief. I felt overcome, bent forward and vomited – right there, in the street, with everyone watching. I felt wretched. I had travelled all this way in the hope of exchanging the box for enough money to travel on. And now I'd lost it! I didn't know what to do. I looked in my bag for a tissue to wipe my mouth. My money came out with it. At least I'd still got that!

I began to feel a bit calmer – to think straight. I needed a plan. I decided the only thing to do was to carry on as if I still had the box – to go to the meeting as planned and try and explain what had happened. Yes, that was the only thing that made sense.

I looked out the address that the man from Acme Couriers had scribbled on the envelope he had given to me in San Francisco. I poked at the faded street map and eventually found it. It wasn't far – I could walk it in next to no time. I wiped my mouth, found a dirty public convenience and washed myself as well as I could. An old woman at the entrance demanded money. I gave her a dollar bill which seemed to satisfy her. I felt much better when I emerged. Everything looked good again.

The streets were full of people, the shops were bright and everywhere cafés spread out over the pavements.

Elegant tanned women lounged back in wicker chairs smoking cigarettes and drinking wine. Most of them wore short skirts; I could not take my eyes off their long thighs – one folded over the other, both coming together in a delightful point which hinted at the beautiful crack which lay at their centre. Men leant forward and held their hands, made suggestions, ran their fingertips along their taut thighs, seeking that delectable point – wanting to probe it, to lick it, to drive their cocks into it, to fill it with their semen. I watched their flattering advances, their hungry eyes and sensed their appetite and heat.

I passed an alley and saw a woman being pressed against a wall by a man. Her light blue skirt was pushed up around her hips, her white blouse pulled down so that both her breasts were bared. The man thrust his cock into her cunt as she entwined his hips with one of her long legs.

I hung back on the corner – watching, licking my lips, fighting against the urge to run my finger along my cunt; realising it was a battle with myself I could not win.

I moved off the main street into the alley and stood behind a large galvanised waste bin that had been turned on its side. The woman was shouting out in joy. She lifted her other leg and rested her weight on the man's hips. He lifted her with his thrusts. She clung to his neck, licking his forehead, staring ahead with glazed passion-filled eyes, gulping with each jarring heave as he penetrated her ever deeper, filled her ever fuller.

I listened to people passing by in the street. None of them were aware of what was happening in the alley, none of them knew that I was watching this man and woman, none of them knew that I could not resist releasing my own passion – that the brief battle with myself was now completely lost.

My excitement overcame me; my mind became

confused. I didn't know what was happening. For a second I thought of going up to the man and woman. It was ridiculous. I saw myself asking the woman if I could take her place, pressing myself back against the wall while the man pushed his heavy cock into my wet cunt. I imagined what she would say, how she would lift herself down, how she would smile graciously and step aside. Perhaps she would help me take off my skirt, perhaps he would prefer I keep it on. I thought of her standing by me, watching, holding my hand, squeezing it in time with my cries of joy as I climbed up higher on his cock. I thought of my body weight dropping down on the shaft, the base of it pressuring against my cunt, bruising the flesh, tugging at it when it withdrew before pounding in again with overbearing strength.

Yes, I could feel every inch of it, every vein on its pulsating surface. I could feel its heat, its power, its burgeoning tip, its swelling mass. I saw myself being lifted off it, the woman helping to hold me up against the wall. I saw myself gasping for breath, and I saw myself being lowered again. This time the massive cock was pressing against my anus, opening it, entering it, then, as it felt the tightening pressure around its end, thrusting deeply inside. I screamed and cried out – filled with the delightful union of pain and pleasure. It was so deep! And so big! I felt as if I was full to the gullet, stuffed completely, overcome by my whole weight bearing down on the heavy mass of the man's stiff and powerful cock.

I couldn't imagine how long it would go on – maybe hours, maybe until I was so sore I had to be laid on the floor to recover, I don't know. I imagined the woman bending to me, licking me, offering me her nipples to suck, anything to bring me around, anything to bring me back from the land of the dead to the world of the living. And I knew it would not be enough, even the succulent nipple in my mouth, the woman's firm breasts, her licking tongue and soft full lips were not enough to allow me to recover. I needed more and she knew it. I could see in her eyes a deeper yearning, a more desperate hunger, one that could not be fulfilled by licking up the wetness of my cunt. It was a deeper need, something more primitive, part of the primeval force of the earth, part of its ancient core, part of the very essence of life, of what life itself depended on – it was all of those things; it was the hunger for blood. It was the yearning to be nourished by that which gave life – the red essence which runs in the veins of every human being. This venous blood was the source of her hunger. Blood which has circulated the body, which carried its oxygen to all the body's parts was what drove her need. Blood that had transmitted its essential food and now flowed with the contact it had made with all that was the living being in which it coursed, blood now ready to travel again into the world of air, to be reinvigorated and make its journey again – that was her need. This was what I saw in her eyes – her hunger for only this.

Would she feed from me or me from her? I didn't know. I didn't think I had the strength to take her blood. I didn't think I had the strength to bite into her flesh, to bury my teeth into her, to suck and draw out her blood. But I must. It was me that needed the strength; it was me that needed the nourishment of her fluid. If she took from me then I would expire – perhaps never to regain consciousness again. If she took from me then I would be cast into an oblivion of unknowing – living eternally and yet never knowing of my existence; the most horrific of fates. No, I must feed on her. Somehow, I must find the strength to take some of her life. She would wait until I was stronger to feed from me. Yes, she would crouch naked at my feet waiting until I was sufficiently revived before she drank from my pulsating veins.

She knew this, of course. She would offer herself first. She would lie beside me, still panting from her own efforts. She would pull her skirt and blouse off so that she was naked. She would stretch out her arms so that her neck was easily accessible, so that I didn't have to move too much to get to it, so that I didn't have to use too much of my slackening strength to find the place of renewal.

I could taste it now – on my lips, in the alley, watching, knowing of her presence, I could taste her on my lips. Her skin would be so sweet, so clean and pure. I would press my mouth against it for a while – just enjoying contact with it, simply savouring its satiny surface. I would feel the beating of her heart even with the lightest touch of my lips. In the end, I would open my mouth. I would not be able to hold back any longer. But still I would be on the verge, on the edge of the wonderful promise of becoming. I would be filled to the brim with the excitement of anticipation – of knowing what was about to happen – but I would not be able to stop it overflowing and in the end would not be able to stop being overwhelmed by its need.

I leant against the alley wall. A deep and penetrating thrill passed through me. I was there, on the cusp, on the edge of the next moment, sensing the pleasures that it would contain, powerless to prevent its coming – a victim of my own terrible prescribed fate.

I could feel the points of my hollowed out canine teeth against her skin. I could feel their sharpness pressing into it – pressing it down, dishing it, testing its elasticity, its tension. I could feel the sustained pressure; I could sense that it would break through the barrier if I kept it up. I sensed the pulsating vein beneath, throbbing against my lips, inviting me, drawing me on. When would I decide to release it? How much longer could I exist on this boundary of expectation? No longer. The skin would break, suddenly opening itself up to me, allowing my teeth to press into the soft tissue, to find the vein, to puncture it, to draw its flowing contents into my hungry mouth. At last, all the potential would be released, my life would be complete, I would be nourished and renewed. I would drink my fill.

Oh, and the taste! Thick and creamy, lacking in oxygen, already used by its owner, already depleted but containing everything I needed – the power of the body, the knowledge of its every part contained in its corpuscles, waiting to be eaten. It had flowed completely through her; it had taken its breath to every corner of her body and had picked up nourishment of a different sort, the power of her being. I feasted on it, right there, in my mind, as I watched her rising time and again on the thrusting cock that filled her with so much pleasure. Yes, her blood, I could see myself devouring it, eating the delicious fluid that ran with her vital power. I could feel it entering my own body, lining my stomach, running into my intestines, filling my organs, seeping into every part of me, giving me the power of another, setting itself into my own flesh, breeding inside me, satisfying my eternal existence with the power to withstand death, the strength to take more and forever replenish myself.

I realised my fingers were deep inside my cunt. I realised I was being watched – two men from the street had seen me and had walked into the alley. A shiver of excitement went through me. But it wasn't a thrill of fear or embarrassment; it was a thrill of expectation and anticipation. Straight away, I knew I wanted them to watch me, to see me. I was overcome with the need for them. I wanted to tell them what I was thinking, what I was imagining. I wanted them to know that I could only be satisfied if I drank the blood of another, fed on it, was nourished by it, replenished by it.

I didn't stop to think. I bent over in front of them. I felt a need for punishment too. Perhaps I felt guilty about what had I had been thinking? I don't know. I just hoped they would realise I needed to feel pain, to feel something that would drive my other desires away, if only for a while. My mind was too confused by it all. I just wanted to be hurt – to feel my body saturated with pain.

I raised my bottom and lifted my skirt. I didn't know what they would do – it didn't matter. I waited – panting, hoping, eager for what I needed. I closed my eyes for a moment. I listened to the woman still crying out in delight as the man continued to thrust her against the dirty brick wall. The sound only inflamed me more. I couldn't get the images of bloodlust out of my mind – I was overtaken by them, overwhelmed by them, lost to their power and control. The only pictures in my head were red, flowing, hot, and saturating.

It was foolish to think they would simply spank me, foolish to imagine they would just bring their hands down against my bottom – smacking it, stinging it, filling me with the simple delight of clear pain. Yes, it was so foolish, but that was what I had been thinking, somewhere in my confusion that was what I had imagined.

I felt hands around my hips. Still, I thought it was a prelude to the spanking. Perhaps they were placing me exactly where they wanted me, making sure their hands would fall flatly against my taut skin? Yes, that was it. But I was wrong. They were not intent on providing me with exactly what I had in my mind – they were intent on fulfilling only their own pleasure, and eagerly, and roughly and without any consideration for me or for any of my desires. At the same moment that I realised this, I felt a wave of darkness come over me – a feeling of the unknown, the danger of it, the presence of evil. I was filled with a naked sense of terrible foreboding.

They flung me down face forward in the alley. I don't know if the man or woman were aware of what was happening – I doubt it, I could still just hear the woman's cries, building to a crescendo but still not released. One of the men held my legs apart, the other lifted my skirt – it was so short it barely covered my bottom anyway. I had no panties on, my cunt was wet. I felt desperately exposed. I didn't know what was going to happen. I tensed myself. I brought my buttocks together. I tightened my thighs. But it was pointless – they were too strong, too determined, too committed to their own purpose.

It was so brutal! So terrifying! I didn't know what was happening to start with – which way I was being pulled, how the pain I was feeling was being inflicted. My mind was in turmoil. I felt giddy and wasn't sure whether I was on my back or face down on my front. I felt as if I was being spun around, twisted – turned in every direction. I saw images – confused and frightening – but they didn't make any sense. I heard the woman's cries, but they were fragmented, broken by the sound of my own gasps, my own panicky gulping.

I felt as if I was whirling through space. Then I knew I was face down, pressed against the dirty damp ground. I smelled the mould in the alley – rotting rubbish, half empty dustbins, discarded clothing. I tasted it against my lips – human debris, detritus from the erosion of human flesh. Its heady acrid stench filled my nostrils. I felt trapped by evil in a place of evil – overcome by darkness in the darkest of places.

They pulled me up by my ankles, dragged me across the filthy cobbles, rubbed the stinking stench that stuck to them onto my skin, my face, my lips. I shouted out. My voice sounded hollow and empty – as if it belonged to another, as if it was merely an echo of a plaintive cry from the past. I felt the pressure of their hands around my ankles. I imagined being dangled from them, bound to a rock and held over a gaping precipice. I felt slapping hands against my bottom – stinging pain, penetrating me, hurting me. Then it spread to my hands, my fingertips and from there it dissipated like sparks from my fingernails.

I realised what was happening when I felt smooth metal against my chest. I still had my blouse on but it was thin and the coldness that emanated from the smooth surface struck me as if I had been flung into an icy pool. They draped me over it so that my full weight was against it. I lay there. Panting, realising my situation, bent forward over the large galvanised waste bin that lay on its side in the alley.

For a moment I thought of the woman and the man. I wondered again if they could see me – if now they were watching me instead of me watching them. I wondered if the woman was still plunging up and down on the man's cock, and the sight of me only excited her more. I imagined her clinging onto the man's neck, staring at me as I lay curved over the heavy waste bin, my bottom already exposed, victim to whatever my tormentors decided would be my fate. I imagined her spit running freely from her mouth, dripping over the man's hair. I pictured her rubbing her face in it, wetting her cheeks, drawing it up her nostrils, thinking of it as his semen, driving herself down hard, riding him, sucking at his cock, eager for its product, fervent for the heat of his fluid.

They were wrapping something around my wrists. I could feel it cutting into my skin, like thin twine or leather thongs. They pulled my arms forward around the large metal bin. I felt squashed against its cold smooth surface. Then I felt them putting something around my ankles – it cut into my skin like the thin twine around my wrists. They splayed my legs so that they would pull forward in line with the cylindrical curve of the bin. I felt the icy coldness of the galvanized metal against the insides of my thighs. They pulled on my wrists and ankles; I pulled against the pressure and felt the same movement in my ankles. Somehow, they had laced my ankles to my wrists – they had led the twine beneath the waste bin and pulled me down firmly against it. I pulled again on my wrists; the pressure on my ankles was instantaneous – it was drawn that tight.

I could feel my heart beating against the hollow metal bin – it echoed inside it, as if my heart itself was empty or had been torn live from my chest and flung into the waste bin. They pulled my head to one side, yanking at my hair until they had it at the angle they wanted. The waste bin rocked forward and back. I felt giddy and tasted heaving vomit in my throat.

There was a pause. I was sure I heard the woman again – groaning, crying out, and groaning again. I thought of her in the final throws of her ecstasy, gripping the man's head in her arms, pressing down, jerking, allowing her orgasm to flow, being overcome by it, drowned by it. I imagined her eyes – wide and staring, declaring that for those few moments she no longer inhabited her body, for those few moments she was transported to another place where nothing lived, nothing died and nothing but ecstasy existed.

Hands forced open my mouth – pulling at my lower jaw, prising it open until it ached. I thought they would press a ball in my mouth, stuff me with it, but instead I felt the heat of a cock – a massive hot swollen cock. It plugged me completely. The glans wedged between my teeth at first then it squeezed in only to be locked there as it swelled up behind my teeth. My lips were stretched so wide they were numb.

I gulped and fought for breath. I tried to shake my head, to escape the stuffing cock in my mouth, but my head was being held fast, pressed against the waste bin by powerful hands, crushing me against it, preventing me from moving at all. I was completely captive, held against the heavy metal cylinder by the twine around my wrists and ankles, my head held fast, my mouth plugged by the massive hot cock.

It would not go any further into my mouth, it touched the back of my throat as it swelled but it would not go down. It simply expanded, pressing my tongue down against the floor of my mouth, squeezing against my cheeks, pressuring against the roof of my mouth.

I felt pain. I reacted but I don't know how – it was impossible to move. I could only imagine how my body wanted to respond – pulling back, tensing, pulling away from the source of the pain. I soaked it up. It started against the taut exposed skin of my buttocks – where they were struck – and flowed into my cunt, my anus and then into the rest of my body. It was a pure pain, uncorrupted by any movement or response, it was simply pain.

Another and another, and the sensation was the same – clear and undiluted pain, stinging, deep and totally penetrating. Another, and yet another. I could not bite down on the cock in my mouth – my jaw was forced too wide. I could not pull my wrists away – if I tried they only pulled against my ankles. I could not yell out, or cry for mercy. I could hardly think. I could only see the pictures in my mind of the woman, groaning and dribbling as she jerked unendingly on the still thrusting cock that was pressed so deeply inside her open wet cunt. And this I could only see through a cloudy haze of red.

I thought I felt hot breath against the stretched side of my neck – an open mouth, a tongue licking, the sharp points of teeth pulling against the skin. Yes, it was a mouth – I could hear the breath – slow and considered, even, unhurried. I felt the teeth against my skin – pressing against it, their tips so sharp. Then another smack across my bottom – so hard, so painful, so penetrating. I was filled with it and with the cock in my mouth. Suddenly, nothing felt right. I felt confused, puzzled. Who was smacking me? I imagined it must be the woman; she must have climbed from the man, her cunt still dripping with his semen. She must be standing behind me, under the instructions of the two men. They must be telling her what to do – when to spank me, when to bring down her hand, when to inflict the next pure pain. Yes, it must be the woman. Perhaps the man was on his knees between her legs licking her dripping cunt, sucking up his own semen, keeping her wetness on his lips so that he would not forget her scent.

Suddenly, I felt the bite in my neck – it was sharp and certain, it cut straight through my skin. I felt the suction against my vein. I felt my blood flowing out of me and into him. I heard his mouth lapping, sucking, then all I felt was the pressure, the flow, the loss. My heart was beating so fast – as if it was excited by the draining, as if it knew I was giving my essence, as if it knew I was being emptied.

The smacking continued, my mouth stayed plugged. I breathed in heavily through my nostrils. I could not change what was happening. I thought of the woman again – beating me in time with the rhythmic sucking at my neck. I thought of her cunt, her beautiful wet cunt, and I slipped into darkness with the scent of her in my nostrils and the red shrouded picture of her in my mind.

I shivered all over – that was the next thing I knew. I had been freed from the waste bin. I was naked. My dress was thrown down like a rag behind it. My jaw ached, my bottom felt on fire – I could hardly touch it. I held my hand against my neck. Yes, my blood had been taken. The raised punctures in my skin testified to that. I felt light headed. I leant against the wall near the entrance to the alley. My heart was beating fast, as if it was struggling to pump my blood around, as if there was not enough for it to work properly. I felt its craving – for more. I pulled my dress on. It was crumpled and dirty. I stumbled out into the street and sat on a bench until I felt strong enough to continue.

Still shaky, I found my way to the address easily. It was a cheap hotel called "East-East" on a side street off the main square. Red geraniums trailed from window boxes beneath the bedroom windows, cascading their harsh scent onto the single canopied table and chairs which waited for diners at the front door. It was quaint on the outside, austere on the inside – dark brown wooden surfaces, drawn curtains, no light, a pervading smell of polish.

The girl behind the reception desk spoke heavily accented English.

When I gave my name, she looked at me inquisitively, and then reached for something from beneath her desk.

'You, Miss Baund. You have message here waiting.'

I took the envelope. It was a scrawled message: "8.30pm, Main Square, outside Café Foil."

I thanked the girl, went to my room, lay on the brown shiny eiderdown that covered the double bed and immediately fell asleep.

The next thing I knew I heard voices outside the window. I got up bleary eyed. I staggered to the window, hardly able to rouse myself. Below, in the alley, people were gathering together, deciding where to go for the evening, and arguing about how to get there. It was nearly 8.30!

I rushed down into the alley and straight to the main square – Hlavné Námestie. It was packed with people, noisy and bustling. All the cafés had chairs and tables spread out over the pavements and into the square. At its centre the Maximilian Fountain spilled out plumes of sparkling water. It reminded me of Vienna – heavy and overbuilt. Street lights lit in the early evening sunlight made it seem darker than it was. I looked for the names above the cafés. It was all a blur. At last I saw it – "Café Foil". I rushed over to it and looked into a sea of faces. I saw a spare chair and sat down. Three other people at the table looked annoyed at my intrusion, staring at me reprovingly before finally carrying on chatting.

I looked around. How would I find the person I needed to contact in this crowd? Or how would they find me? How could we ever recognise each other?

I saw a man walking in my direction – he was tall. I couldn't quite make out his face against the lights that surrounded the pavement terrace of chairs and tables. He came closer. There was something about him that seemed familiar. No, it was impossible! He stepped out of the shadow of the lights and stood by my side. The others at the table said hello to him – they clearly knew him. It was Pastor Wick!

8. SPARKY

Pastor Wick! I couldn't believe it! The last I'd seen of him he'd been running behind me in the jet way when I boarded the plane at San Francisco. I didn't know what to think. Why was he here? Was he still pursuing me? Did he still want to take me back to Pacific Heights? Pacific Heights! That seemed an age ago! Yes, of course, that was it. He was trying to get me back to that dreadful place, to service his flock!

I stared at him blankly.

He ordered a drink and asked me casually what I wanted.

'Something to eat would be good,' I said nervously, not knowing what else to do or say. As I said it I felt ridiculous.

'Choose what you want. It's been a long journey. You deserve it as well, for all your effort.'

'Just a salad. That'll do fine.'

My words sounded completely absurd. How could I be talking like this?

'You look surprised to see me.'

'Well...yes...I am.'

He laughed.

'You didn't make the connection! Of course! How amusing. Oh, Syra!'

I didn't know what he meant.

'Sorry?'

'Don't you understand, Syra? Why do you think I'm here? Do you think I have emerged out of nowhere? Do you think I'm a ghost? Do you think our meeting is a coincidence? Syra, your appointment is with me! I'm the one you have travelled all this way to meet. Well, actually, I'm standing in, so to speak, for the one who had originally planned to meet you. I'm afraid she could not make it! Now, do you have the package that was entrusted to you? Syra, the package? Perhaps you would be kind enough to hand over the package now.'

My heart was pounding. It was only slowly sinking in what was happening. Of course, he couldn't have been the one I was meant to meet! That was impossible. How could it be him?

'Where is the person I was supposed to meet?'

I looked around as if somehow the right person would appear and make themselves known.

'Delayed, I'm afraid – *permanently* delayed.'

He laughed and swigged his drink – an opaque pink mixture with salt encrusted around the edge of the bowl shaped glass. The white ring around his neck showed prominently. Two puncture marks on the right hand side made me shiver as I was reminded again of Pacific Heights, of the flock and of Pastor Wick's mission to bring me to them.

"*Permanently* delayed" – he made it sound so ominous.

He licked the salt from his lips as he placed the glass back carefully on the table.

'I need salt in this heat – lots of it. Now, the box? Syra, perhaps you would give me the box?'

'I'm afraid...I'm afraid...I don't have it.'

He laughed as he twirled the glass slowly in his hand and licked all the salt from around the rim.

'This is some kind of silly joke, isn't it?'

'No, it's not. It was stolen. I don't have it, and I don't have enough money to get out of this place.'

He stared hard at me. I could see he was enraged and barely managing to hold it back.

'Syra, I'm not interested in your jokes. Now! Hand over the box!'

'It's not a joke! It's the truth! I don't have it!'

'Tell me where it is, Syra. I don't want to play silly games. Just tell me where it is.'

His face was reddening as he struggled to keep calm.

'I don't know. It was stolen. It's the truth.'

'Stolen! Syra, my patience is running out. I want the box you were given in San Francisco. I'm not interested in this nonsense. Just tell me where it is.'

I could see he was unable to restrain his anger much longer, but I didn't know what else to say.

'Two girls took it! They just ran away with it! At the station! It's the truth – '

'Syra, just tell me where the box is. It will be better for you in the long run.'

His voice was quivering.

'I have. It's gone. That the truth!'

His face was red with anger. He leant across the table and took hold of my arm. I could feel his pulse beating hard in his fingers as they wrapped tightly around my wrist. He squeezed it tightly in a vice like grip.

'Syra, I have been patient, I have tried hard to be patient, you are, after all, important to the flock – very important – but the box is very important to us as well, more important than you know. Syra, the box is *very* important to us. I must have the box.'

'I'm telling you the truth. It was stolen.'

He pinched the skin of my forearm between his finger and thumb. I bit my lips, trying to hold back the pain. He squeezed harder. I thought my arm was going to break. He twisted his hand around my arm, pulling at my skin, burning me. I gasped for breath. Suddenly, with his other hand he grabbed my bag and tore it open. He pulled out my passport and held it up in front of me.

I felt as if my heart had stopped. I gasped for breath.

'You went to a lot of trouble to get this the last time, I recall. I'm sure you'll go to just as much trouble this time.' He waved the passport in front of my face. 'I'll keep this for a few days, just so that you have something to think about while you find me the box. I'm sure it will help you in your search. Yes, I'm sure you'll find the *stolen* box more easily now. I'll see you here, the day after tomorrow, same time. You'll give me the box, you can have your passport back, and then we'll travel back to your true home together. The flock will welcome you with open arms. Just think, Syra, you will be able to feed them and bring others into our world. Syra, just think, your life will then be complete.'

He thrust the passport into his trouser pocket, let go of my arm got up and dashed away across the crowded café.

For a moment, I did nothing – I was too confused, too filled with fear. My arm was burning from his twisting grip. The sound of voices around me filled my head like the beating of a drum. Then I went into a panic as I realised he had run away with my passport!

I jumped up and ran after him. I knocked over a chair and spilled a tray of drinks a young female waiter was carrying to a group of men on the edge of the sprawl of chairs and tables that reached out into the square. I apologised as I ran flustered across the square and into a narrow street that led off alongside a huge heavy walled building.

The street was dark. It was suddenly quiet – the massive stone walls of the building seemed to soak up all sound. For a moment I couldn't make anything out. The dim yellow street lamps shed pools of light along its length. Pastor Wick ran from one to the next like a fleeing wraith escaping the exposure of the dark and seeking the sanctuary of the day. I just ran after him, not thinking what I would do if I caught him up, not thinking that I would be better to run away, to put it all behind me and escape. All I could see in my mind was my passport in his hand. All I could feel inside myself was the fear of being without it.

He seemed to jump from each puddle of light to the next. It was as if he flew between them – alighting on them like a fly, eyeing up his next target then flinging himself towards it before moving on again.

The walls narrowed, the cobbled street tightened, two heavy, cast iron bollards blocked the way to traffic. Pastor Wick mounted the top of one of them and crouched there, peering around him, swinging his arms by his side, perfectly balanced and poised.

I stopped. Seized with sudden fear, frozen with the terrible idea that I might catch him up and that he would challenge me, throw me to the ground and feed on me, then carry me off in his arms and discard me in the river. I imagined myself floating down the grey blue Danube, my throat pierced, bleeding profusely, staining the waters as Pastor Wick buzzed above me gloating and dripping his bloodstained saliva over my face.

He leapt to another bollard. I saw his face in the murky light – grey, drawn, his mouth open, his teeth bared, glittering spit running over his bottom lip. He had transformed into something terrible, something animal-like, a terrible corruption of humanity. His eyes were wide – yellow, penetrating, seeing into another world, or staring out from one. He dropped to the ground from the bollard. He ran forward still in a crouch, running the flats of his hands along the cobbles as though contact with them gave him a strange other-worldly pleasure. He dodged from side to side as he ran, at first glancing the walls of the narrow street, then hitting them harder, pushing against them, then finally climbing up their sides and running along the vertical walls as though they were horizontal surfaces.

I couldn't believe what I was seeing. I still pursued him, but now it was like running forward in a dream – I was making no progress no matter how much I tried.

The street narrowed more. He jumped from one side to the other, clinging to the walls like a spider, looking around for threats, for victims, or someone that was following him!

Suddenly, I realised I was in danger – if he should turn back and see me, if he should scent me in his wide nostrils, if he should smell my blood!

There was an entrance ahead. I saw a flashing neon sign dangling above a dimly lit door – "Club Lichvář".

Pastor Wick sprang to the ground. He looked back quickly – only for a second – then in an instant he was through the door and it closed behind him.

I still felt as if my feet were stuck in glue. I struggled forward, reaching out for the door, keeping my eyes fixed on the blue and red flashing sign that dangled above it.

When finally I reached it I was gasping for breath.

Two girls stood beneath the flashing light. I had not seen them when Pastor Wick disappeared through the door. One wore pink tights, a black tight vest top and a spiky hemmed mesh skirt with glittering stars hanging from the spikes. Her hair was bright red and roughed up in a wild tangle. The other one had a puffed out mesh skirt that barely covered her hips, a cross over black top, pink panties, tall pink socks and white plimsolls. Her hair was dyed white and her bright red lipstick stood out against her pale smooth skinned face. Both of them were dodging between customers that had suddenly arrived at the club entrance. They took their hands, offered them tickets, laughed with them, pushed at them, joked, engaged their attention completely. They both moved so quickly – like beautiful moths caught in the glare of the neon light that entranced them so much they could not escape its captivity.

I couldn't understand how Pastor Wick had disappeared so quickly. I couldn't understand what I had seen – his strange clawing progress, clinging to walls, jumping from side to side like an animal. And now, these strange beautiful girls, and their energy and focus.

Still unable to hold myself back, I went up to the entrance.

The girl with the white hair came straight up to me. She spoke quickly in English, flashing from one subject to the other, full of energy, packed with interest, unable to rest on something for more than a second at a time. She was like an excited butterfly dodging from flower to flower, never sufficiently nourished, never completely satisfied.

'My name's Sparky,' she said. 'Don't you think my English is good? I studied it at school. It was my favourite subject – that and Latin. This is my friend Anicka. What's your name? I bet I can guess. Go on. Let me guess! Let me see. I think it's...its...'

'Syra.'

'I was just going to say that! I knew it! Syra! Syra! What a beautiful name. Syra and Sparky! How exciting!'

'I'm looking for someone – a man. He was just ahead of me. He ran through here, only a minute ago.'

'A lost soul eh?' she said, nodding and scratching her chin in a forced dramatic way. 'Anicka! Have we seen any lost souls in the last few minutes?'

Anicka giggled and nodded. She ran up close and grabbed hold of Sparky's hand. They cuddled briefly then kissed each other fully on the mouth. Sparky raised herself onto tiptoes, stretching her legs, tightening her thighs and tensing her panty covered bottom. As they parted, Sparky's tongue hung freely over her bottom lip. It glistened with spit in the light of the flashing neon light. Its fleshy pinkness contrasted with the red gash of her lips marked out like a splash of blood against her white face.

Her face was quickly animated – as though she had suddenly been woken from a dream.

'Quick, Anicka! Here's someone for us. Get him. See if he wants to spank me! Anicka! Quick!'

She twirled around, darted a quick smile at me then ran to Anicka's side.

Anicka had grabbed a young man who was just about to enter the club. She blocked his way, holding his hand, curtsying, smiling provocatively, opening her mouth, endearing herself to him. Sparky stood behind her, bobbing up and down, playing hide and seek, giggling and shaking her spiky hair from side to side.

Sparky turned to me and smiled excitedly. Her wide eyes were bright and sparkled with an uncontrollable zest and life.

Anicka pulled the man away from the door, out of the pool of flashing light cast by the neon sign and into the darker part of the narrow cobbled street.

Sparky grabbed my hand and pulled me after them. I didn't know what to expect but the heat of her hand, the darkness of the narrow street, Sparky and Anicka's strange clothing, their excitability and purpose, all filled me with waves of excitement that I couldn't resist.

'Stand here,' said Sparky. 'You'll like it. I promise!'

I did as she said. She grinned, clapped her hands together and bobbed up and down.

'Here,' said Anicka to the man. 'This is a good place.'

She held the man's right hand and rubbed both her hands on either side of it.

'There,' she said. 'I'll warm it up for you.'

Sparky stood in front of them both, giggled and bowed low before turning and bending forward. She turned back and grinned at me as she pulled down her pink panties to the middle of her thighs. She spread her fingers and placed the palms of her hands around her knees. Her bottom was tight and smooth. Her skin was pale. At the base of the crack of her buttocks I could just make out the darkness that shadowed her cunt. She pushed her bottom up higher and I could see the fine crack at its centre but still not clearly.

'There!' said Anicka to the man. 'That'll be twenty dollars.'

The man looked at her quizzically.

'Four hundred crowns.'

He pulled some money out of his pocket and counted it out into her hand.

All the time Sparky stayed completely still, her pink panties midway down her thighs, her pink socks defining the perfect shape of her slim calves, the loosely tied laces of her white plimsolls dangling on the ground.

When the money had been handed over, Anicka moved back and the man stood behind Sparky. He rubbed his hand slowly across her bottom. Still she did not move. He ran his forefinger along the crack between her buttocks and down the insides of her thighs. He gripped her pink panties and twisted them. I thought she would tighten her legs in response to the increased pressure but still she did not move.

He stood back and moved slightly to the side. He looked at her bottom for a minute or two – savouring its shape, its tightness, its readiness. He stared at her panties – twisted up around her thighs – and he looked at her tight pulled socks and contrasting white plimsolls. He absorbed the beauty of her, the undefended exposure of her.

I realised I was licking my lips – they had become dry as I watched her.

He drew his hand back and without stopping at the top of the arc brought it down swiftly.

I watched his flat spread hand getting closer to her bottom. It seemed to take an age – as if it was in slow motion, out of step with time. When it finally made contact it seemed to stick to her skin. Her bottom was elastic – giving slightly under the weight of his hand as it struck then bouncing back straight away. But his palm stuck to it, holding in the pain it inflicted, not letting it escape. When he pulled it away it was only to draw it back straightaway and bring it down again. This time I heard the slapping sound of its contact, this time I heard Sparky catch her breath. He repeated the process. Rhythmically, he brought it down again and again. I heard her gasp, though I couldn't tell whether it was an intake of breath or an exhalation. I saw her biting her lips. I could see that the pain of the slapping hand was driving itself deeper, that she was struggling to withstand it in silence.

Again he brought it down, again she gasped, again I saw her biting her lips.

Suddenly, she moved one of her hands. It was quick – like a twitch, a cramp, a muscular spasm. She brought it around and covered her bottom with it – her fingers spread out wide, her pink painted nails glistening from the flickering neon light.

The man stopped, his arm held high – frozen with surprise and annoyance.

He scowled at Anicka but did not speak. She understood his unspoken message.

'I'm so sorry,' she said. 'So sorry. It's okay, it won't happen again.'

She bent her mouth to Sparky's ear.

'Sparky,' she said. 'Sparky, you must not move. You know that. Sparky! Four hundred crowns! Two hundred each!'

She took hold of Sparky's hand and pulled it away. Sparky replaced it back over her knee.

Anicka turned to the man, his hand still frozen at the top of its arc.

'It'll be alright now. I promise. Please carry on. There won't be any more problems.'

The man nodded then brought his hand down again. The blow knocked the breath from Sparky. I saw her fighting to keep still – struggling to hold in the pain, battling to stop her hand coming up to protect herself again.

The next time his hand smacked down it was so hard she rocked forward. I thought she was going to lose her balance but she managed to retain it and stay in place. The next blow knocked her forward again and this time she had to put her foot out to stop herself from falling over. She trod on one of the dangling laces and I thought she was going to trip over.

She brought herself back into position quickly but it had obviously annoyed the man – still angry from the first disobedience. He grabbed her pink panties and pulled them down to behind her knees. It was a sign of his anger. He brought his fingers up between her thighs and pressed them hard into the dark crevice of her cunt. He lifted her on them, widening the crack of her buttocks, exposing the shape of her delectable slit. He held her there for a while – testing her, seeing if she would react against him, resist him, try to stop him.

I could see the moisture of her cunt on his fingers as he pulled them away. I could see she was trembling – from fear or excitement, frustration or aggravation, it was impossible to tell.

Just as his hand was coming down again she once more brought her own hand around and placed it in the way.

My stomach filled with nerves.

He stopped half way – suddenly, as if his hand had hit an invisible wall. I could feel anger emanating from him in invisible waves.

Anicka hurried forward and grabbed Sparky's hands. Frantically, she pulled them back onto her knees, produced a thin ribbon and began binding them tightly in place. She wound it around several times then knotted it tightly. The loose ends dangled down against Sparky's ankles.

Anicka stood back and nodded keenly to the man, telling him it was alright to continue but not daring to speak.

The next time the man brought his hand down Sparky cried out but she did not move – it was impossible, she was tied too tightly with the ribbon. She rocked forward with the next blow but did not try to stop herself falling – she kept her feet close together, hoping that she would not drop forward and lose her balance. Her bottom began to redden – a broad smear across her pale smooth skin. I imagined how much it must be stinging.

I stood there watching as the punishment continued. I didn't know how long it would go on – how long it *could* go on. Sparky was screaming loudly now. Every time the man's hand landed on her upturned bottom she cried out louder than the time before. To start with they were gasps, then they became whimpers, then they formed into cries, then into screams. As the screams became more intense she started to beg for the punishment to stop.

'Please!' 'Please!' she shouted out each time his hand came down. 'It hurts too much! I can't take any more!' she screeched in the short gap between the blows – punctuating her simple cries for mercy with proclamations of her pain and need for relief.

For a while, he did not complain, perhaps enjoying her cries of pain and her begging appeals for an end to it all. After a while though, her hands became loose in her bonds and she could not prevent herself from moving them. He stopped again and scowled at Anicka. Anicka took the spare ends of the ribbon and tightened Sparky's hands more firmly to her knees. When Anicka stood back and nodded, the man continued.

He stopped again, ran his hands between her legs and pulled at the front of her cross over black top. He dragged it down off her shoulders and exposed her breasts – they were small and pert, her nipples pink and hard. She whimpered as he did it and I watched a stream of spit drooling from her open mouth. When he resumed the spanking, spit flew from her mouth in a misty spray as again the breath was forced by pain and suffering from her fragile and anguished body.

I felt so sorry for her. Her bottom was so red, her cries so loud and out of control, her punishment so harsh. I stepped forward, thinking that I should help, perhaps offer myself instead? Anicka glowered at me. I stepped back. I was shivering, shaking all over – with fear or excitement, I couldn't tell.

Anicka produced another ribbon and bound it across Sparky's mouth. She wound it around her head twice – pinching in her cheeks, pinning her tongue inside, silencing her cries and stifling her pleas for mercy or help.

The man continued. I watched but in a way I did not see anything. The only sensations I had were the smacking sounds of the slapping contact his flat hand made against Sparky's reddened bottom. It filled my head – echoing, hollow, fading into the distance before returning again even louder.

Suddenly, my other senses returned.

I looked again at Sparky – still bent over, her panties now around her ankles, her hands bound to her knees, her mouth tied tightly, her punishment continuing. I felt a need to push my fingers into my cunt. I felt a need to take her place. I felt a need to bend down behind her and lick her wet cunt. Yes, I wanted so much to taste the sweetness of her cunt, to press my tongue into the slit, lap at its moisture, inhale its beautiful aroma.

I was squeezing the base of my clitoris, rising up on my hand, as I watched the man take out his cock and drive it into Sparky's anus. She could not yell out any more – she had exhausted herself, exhausted her pain. He thrust her hard and roughly. When he pulled it out, Anicka took it in her hands. She massaged the shaft, drawing out his semen, before going down on her knees before him and sucking at it until her thirst for it was completely satisfied. Sparky stayed where she was, not moving now, her eyes wide, her nostrils inhaling the air she needed to satisfy the demand for oxygen in her racing blood.

I felt confused and lost – everything was spinning around. I could barely stop myself falling as I ran back into the square and crouched down panting on the edge of the massive Maximilian Fountain. I listened to its spurting waters, unable to get the pictures of Sparky out of my mind, unable to stop the waves of joy that kept spreading through my still jerking body.

I walked to a telephone kiosk. I had to try and sort things out. I found the telephone number on a crumpled up piece of paper in the bottom of my bag. I stood in front of the gash blue and yellow telephone. I could hardly read its dim display and couldn't understand its "1-2-3" instructions. After several failed attempts, I finally got through.

'Acme Couriers.'

'It's Syra Bond...in Bratislava. Do you remember? The box?'

'Of course, yes. I hope everything's okay. No problems are there?'

'No...no...not really – '

'Good! For a moment there, I thought you might have lost the package or something stupid like that! I'm mighty relieved to know that things are okay. It's a pretty special package, I can tell you. I've even had the FBI around here since you left. Twice! The first time a woman in a red dress, the next a man and neither of them seemed to know what the other was doing!'

'Yes...yes...things are fine – '

'They wanted to know this and that. I couldn't tell them much – just that it was a heart, going to somewhere for research. That's all I knew. What else could I say?'

I didn't know how to reply.

'I've got to go...sorry...I've got to go...'

'When you've made the delivery contact me again. I've got another job you may be interested in. What do you think of that, eh? A heart in a box!'

'Yes...I'm sorry...yes...'

I left the telephone handset dangling from its cord. I had hardly stepped out of the kiosk when, from nowhere, Sparky ran up behind me and kissed my neck.

9. BLOODLUST

'That's so sweet!' Sparky cried out breathlessly. 'I do like your neck. I do like kissing it! Look I'm by myself. I'm a bit tired of Anicka. She's too fussy about things. I can be your special friend instead. Oh, you look sad.' She pressed the tips of her fingers to her temples, closed her eyes in forced concentration. 'Let me use my powers to work out the problem. Yes, I have it!' She opened her bright eyes wide, grabbed my hands and beamed excitedly. 'I think you have lost something. I can tell. It's my powers. Yes, you have lost something. I'm right aren't I? I'm a real clairvoyant, aren't I? You have, haven't you? I know you have. I can see it in your face. You've no need to reply! Let me help you find it. Let me help you get it back. Tell me I'm right! Tell me! I know I'm right! Tell me! Tell me! How much money do you have? We'll need some for fares. I love going on the trams. Ring-ring! Look, I've got quite a bit. How much have you got? Tell me I'm right! Tell me! Tell me! I'm so excited! We're on an investigation! You *have* lost something haven't you? Tell me! Tell me!'

'Yes, I have. You're right, I have.'

'I'm so pleased. Not pleased that you've lost something, of course, but pleased that I'm right, and that I'm going to help you find it. This is the most exciting thing that's ever happened to me!'

She was a flurry of excitement. She danced around me, ran her outstretched hands against walls, jumped over bollards, and pinched people's cheeks playfully as they passed us in the street. We spent the afternoon walking around the city, sitting at terrace cafés, and staring at people or the river.

Sparky came back with me to the hotel. Without taking her clothes off, she curled up at the bottom of my bed and went to sleep.

The next thing I knew, it was morning. Sparky was still asleep at the bottom of the bed – she looked like a beautiful elf. Her panty covered bottom was taut, and the crease between her buttocks precisely defined. I wanted to run my tongue along it. I wanted to taste the sweetness of her cunt through the silky pink material, I wanted to smell her, to press my eyes and nose against her barely covered flesh, I wanted to inhale her. I reached my hand out and touched the delectable fold of flesh that was squeezed within the gusset between her legs. It was so soft, so perfect. I felt its warmth and, like a jolting shock of electricity, a shivering tingle of excitement ran through me. She was irresistible.

She did not stir as I bent my face towards that delightful crease of her cunt. I felt her sweet flavour in my nostrils. She moved slightly, bringing one leg up higher and pushing the other one down straight. Her soft flesh was squeezed even tighter by the covering of thin material. I looked along the dark valley at its centre, imagining what it covered – the pink slit of her soft, moist cunt.

I reached out and felt the edge of the material – just the touch of it made me tremble with excitement. And the boundary where it met her skin formed the most perfect union. I lifted it slightly away from her skin. My hand was shaking with the thrill of it – seeing her body revealed beneath it, uncovered, exposed. She did not move. I lifted it further. I saw the flesh of her cunt – the soft edge, slightly raised from the centre, flattened at the side. I lifted the material further. I could hardly bear it – my heart was pounding so loudly, my head was thumping. I saw the crack – pink, moist, warm, beckoning. I couldn't imagine anything more faultless. I just wanted to stare at it, absorb it without ever approaching it. But I couldn't hold myself back. I bent my face towards it. I smelled her sweetness – like honey, like new mown hay, like damp spring air in the warming sun. I licked out my tongue. I could taste her before I even touched her with its eager tip. My saliva ran over my lip and dripped onto her cunt. I pulled back, thinking she would be roused by its dewy touch – somehow startled, awoken from her dream. I waited, frozen, my heart thumping, my temples pounding. She did not move.

Finally, I let the tip of my tongue make contact with her flesh. I pulled the material aside, so that I could run it fully along the delectable crack. It opened at the first touch – easily, readily, keenly. Her taste was ambrosia – the very food of the gods. I could not stop my eyes closing – it was as though I was transported to a different world, made unconscious simply being in the presence of its heavenly sweetness.

I don't know how long I licked her cunt – it could have been an hour, a year, it was impossible to tell. She moved occasionally – bringing her leg up higher, opening her legs slightly, moaning once, and once turning her head to the side. At one point she started to stretch but stopped just as she began bending her elbows. I thought of her bending down in the narrow street outside the club – so keen, so eager for punishment. I thought of spanking her myself. I imagined turning her over the end of the bed now, pressing her face down on the brown shiny eiderdown, pulling her panties down, exposing her bottom, checking all the time that she was still asleep. I imagined rubbing my hand across the cheeks of her bare bottom – feeling their tautness, their heat, their elasticity. I wondered when I would first bring my hand down. I knew that as soon as I did she would wake and then the spell would be broken. I pictured myself holding my hand high above her bottom – waiting, expecting, anticipating, all the time bringing fulfilment into the present but never allowing it to be released. Then, unable to hold back, I saw myself bringing it down with a sudden hard slap.

The sound echoed in my ears. I knew then that the magic would be broken; she would wake and turn and cry out. Perhaps she would allow herself to be spanked, but it would be different now that she was awake. The sense of anticipation would be replaced by a different pleasure – I would know her pleasure, I would see it in her face, hear it in her sobs and cries, feel it in the twitching of her anguished body. But then I saw that she did not wake, that she stayed asleep, unconscious, unaware of my spanking hand, of her punishment, and, as I realised this, my heart pounded so wildly I thought it would burst and my stomach filled with an overpowering nervous excitement that threatened to consume me hungrily from within.

Then I realised it was really happening. This was not just in my mind, it was actually happening. I saw myself bringing my hand down again – watching myself as if in a dream, but this was not a dream. Yes, it was true, and she did not wake! I was spanking her and she was still unconscious of the pain, the slapping sound, the pressure of my hand. I brought it down again, and again. She lay there, bent over the edge of the bed, unconscious, unaware, innocent of the punishment she was receiving at my hand. She made no sound, she did not scream or cry out, she did not even move. I stood back for a moment looking at her reddened buttocks. Her head was turned to the side, her mouth open, the tip of her tongue pressed out beneath her top lip. Her eyes were tightly closed, her spiky white hair radiating from her head like an exploding star against the dark brown cosmos of the shiny eiderdown.

I stripped off my clothing and stood naked. My nipples were hard and throbbing. I felt my own cunt – it was soft and moist, aching along its naked slit. I pressed my fingers into the crack and massaged the yielding flesh. I felt my face flushing with excitement. My anus ached. I wanted it filled with a cock. I wanted to sit down on a heavy stiff cock. I wanted to be crammed full with a pulsating venous shaft deep in my rectum.

I bent forward and continued the spanking. I brought my hand down harder and harder until I felt a constricting tightness in my own hips. A tide of excitement ran between them, heat pulsed through my beating clitoris, tingling burst into my erect nipples. I could not hold back. I did not have the strength to fight against it, and I did not have the strength to continue her punishment. I was overcome and depleted yet still hungry for more. I fell forward onto my knees and lapped at her cunt as my orgasm flowed though me in heavy, seizing waves. The cramping spasms made me gulp and I slurped noisily as I dribbled spit and moisture from my lips and tongue.

I wanted to tie her up as Anicka had done. I needed to tie her up. I pulled at one of the loose laces in her plimsolls and drew it free. I wound it around her wrists. There seemed no point at first – she did not move anyway – but as I pulled the lace tighter, as I watched it digging into her pale skin, as I felt her lack of response or resistance – I realised that binding her was essential. It was taking me to a level of excitement I had never known. It was her lack of resistance that excited me most; that she was so completely inert, unaware of my actions, so unaware of any pain I was inflicting on her. Binding her when she did not move or offer any resistance drew me into a world of pleasure in which I felt I would expire from sheer delight. It was her innocent immobility, her sweet lack of resistance even as she was bound, and the pain I was inflicting even though she knew nothing of it, that overwhelmed me.

I pulled the lace tighter, hardly able to believe that she would not wake up, but she didn't.

I looked at her mouth – slightly open, her lips parted and trembling with each sharp intake of breath. Could I bind her mouth as well? Would it be possible to restrain her from crying out even though she would not cry out?

I could not resist her. I could not resist my desires. I started to pull her white plimsoll from her foot. She stretched her leg slightly. I stopped and waited. She went still again. I drew the plimsoll away. One by one she stretched her toes inside her tightly pulled pink sock. Again I waited, again she went still. I leant across her. I felt her chest rising and falling as she breathed. Her pale stretched neck looked so entrancing. I knew I would like to bite into it, to suck at her veins, to feel the elements of her body that it carried. But first I wanted to stuff her mouth with the plimsoll. I wanted to see it plugged, stopped up, filled.

I opened her mouth a little, putting my fingers on her lower teeth and pulling down her jaw. Her bottom lip quivered slightly. When I thought it was open enough I pushed the rubber covered toe end of the plimsoll in her mouth.

The rubber toecap went straight in. She sucked air in against it, catching her breath for a moment, before relaxing and inhaling heavily through her nostrils. I pushed the plimsoll in further, opening her mouth as wide as I could with my fingers then stuffing it in completely. It forced her mouth wide, stretching it at the corners.

I sat and watched her – bound by the wrists and with her mouth plugged with the plimsoll, unmoving, unguarded, and innocent of what was happening. I bent to her neck. I couldn't resist it – everything seemed right. She looked so peaceful, so submissive, so entrancing.

I kissed her neck, just below her ear. Her spiky haired head rested on the brown bed cover and her neck stretched away from me. It looked so naked, so accessible – that pale passage of her body between her head and her shoulders, the conduit for all her veins, the route to her mind, the pathway for all the commands that carried out her wishes. Her elegant neck – the pathway of all her becoming. I looked at the faint lines of the tendons that controlled her movements, the light blue strips that hinted at the flowing blood beneath, the shallow beating of her pulse given away by the taut pulsating rise and fall beneath her skin. I thought of her heart – pumping out the oxygenated blood to her body, drawing it from her lungs and pressing it into service. I imagined it flowing to every part of her – pounding into her organs, taking power to her limbs, seeping into the most distant and fragile capillaries at the ends of her fingertips and toes. I pictured the blood flowing back – desperate to return to her heart, hungry to be reinvigorated. And that blood, I thought of that more than anything, depleted of strength but carrying the germ of her very existence – that was the blood I thought about, that was the blood I wanted. It was this special blood, this venous blood – lacking pressure, flowing slowly, distant from the pressing pulse of her heart – that I desired. I wanted to taste its rawness, its own hunger, its impregnation of her every part. This was the blood that had touched all of her and become exhausted because of its effort, this was the blood that knew her best and had given of itself to feed her, this was the blood that needed air to survive and continue.

I looked for the place – just below her ear, where the visible beating of her heart corresponded with the light blue vein that travelled beneath it. I opened my mouth and pressed my lips against her taut pale skin. I opened my mouth wider and felt the edges of my teeth making contact with it. The pointed tips of my hollowed out canine teeth pressed against the flesh – they were so sharp, I knew they would puncture it easily. I rested there for a few moments, my heart thumping madly, my head spinning with a mixture of overpowering desire and panic-laden apprehension. Suddenly, I saw what I was doing – lying on the top of this delicate unconscious girl, getting ready to bite into her neck, preparing to suck the blood from her veins. I felt breathless – overcome with anxiety, filled with the horror of it all. I couldn't believe what I was doing! I couldn't believe that my knowledge of it still allowed me to continue!

I pressed my teeth down harder. Each broke the skin at the same time. It was such a deliberate act. I knew I had to dig them deeper to find the vein. I tensed my jaws and began to draw them together. I felt the points of my teeth burying themselves further into Sparky's flesh. I felt her blood oozing into my mouth, mixing with my saliva, lubricating my tongue, introducing me to the feed. Then I felt the vein – pulsating against a tendon. I tightened my jaw more. I felt its shape – soft, not hard walled like an artery, flowing with blood at low pressure; the perfect pressure to feed on. The points of my teeth went into the wall of the vein. I pictured the incision in my mind. The blood flowed straight away. I sucked against it and filled my mouth with it. It ran over my tongue, against the insides of my cheeks, it covered my teeth. It flowed to the back of my throat – already coagulating, already congealing into heavy globs as it mixed with my saliva.

I swallowed hard. I felt its power, the message that it carried of Sparky's body, her life, her very being. All of it was now mine – within me, soaking into my own system, being absorbed into me, needing my oxygen, needing the new life that I could breathe into it.

I sucked more of the flowing blood. I filled myself with it, gulping at it, slavering at it, burrowing my face into the bloody wound, covering myself with Sparky's streaming nectar. I realised my eyes were closed and when I opened them all I could see was tinted red. They were covered with Sparky's blood, covered with a film of redness, tainting the world of my senses with its hue, dyeing everything with the crimson blush of my hunger and lust – red was the colour of everything I needed.

I realised I had my fingers in Sparky's cunt. It was a beautiful place for them to be. I knew when I pulled them out I would sniff them – inhale them deeply – and lick them until the taste of her was fixed forever in my mind. I kept them there as I pulled away and looked at her. Two small streams of blood ran from the wounds in her neck. I watched the flow slacken then cease. Still my eyes were filled with blood, still my fingers were inside her soft wet cunt, and still she was unconscious of me and what I was doing.

10. THE SISTERS

It had been light for hours. I got up and took a shower. The water ran red around me. I felt as if I was standing in a pool of blood. I imagined it soaking up my legs, into my cunt, my breasts, my heart. I didn't know what had happened to me. I felt as if I was some sort of monster.

As I went downstairs I was overcome by a sense of unsolvable confusion. I didn't know which way to turn, what to do next. I couldn't tell what I wanted, what I was doing. My desires felt like fears, my fears like desires. Everything had become so mixed up. It was as though I had caught a disease; as if I had been infected by a germ that my mind could not deal with and my body could not resist. I knew I carried an infection of bloodlust – I had been told that – but I had been told I was immune to its effects. Now it seemed to be taking me over, winning the battle I had not even thought I needed to wage. Yes, I was being overpowered by something I could not understand, beaten by something that was too much for me to resist.

I went into a courtyard behind the hotel. It was shaded by a heavy timber loggia. A beautiful mixture of aromas filled it – cinnamon, coffee, cigar smoke, olive oil, the musky smell of women.

I sat on a shiny metal chair beneath the cascading vines. A good looking young man came to me with a note pad in his hand. I asked for something refreshing. He smiled courteously and went away.

I sat back on the chair – the seat was cool against the backs of my thighs. I stretched my legs out, pushed my shoes off and flexed my toes. I started to feel more relaxed.

I listened to a slow slapping sound, like something tapping against a window in the wind. It stopped the started again. I heard something that sounded like a woman's cry – again regular, keeping time with the tapping sound and dropping back when the tapping sound ceased.

I lifted my right foot onto my left knee. I felt the cool fragrant air against the soft naked flesh of my cunt. I ran my hand down across it, slipping it over the thin material and into the crease of my slit. My knee dropped lower as I found my clitoris and pressed at its base. My buttocks tightened as a surge of joy ran between my hips and up into my chest.

Screened by a broad leaved plant climbing up from a massive purple pot, two young women sat talking intently. I could hear them clearly although their voices were almost in whispers. It was as if a long held secret was passing between them and the importance of it demanded a lower level of sound than communication of the everyday sort. Their clandestine intrigue excited me. I stroked my fingers around the base of my clitoris. The wave of joy passed through my body again as I listened carefully. They were both speaking in English although they were clearly Czech.

I peeped between the leaves of the plant. They were both young but one was older than the other, and darker haired. It was obvious they were sisters; there was something indefinable in their looks which said they were related – their lips maybe, or their eyes; it was impossible to tell, but there was something. The older sister was called Vanya, the younger Jana. They leant towards each other across a small aluminium table. They held each other's hands as though touching made the secret they were sharing that much easier to bear.

The young man came back with my drink on a tray. He placed it in front of me. I pulled my hand away from my cunt and my face flushed red with embarrassment.

He raised his eyebrows and nodded his head towards a window above the courtyard.

'Don't worry,' he said smirking. 'It's always fun here.'

I didn't know what to say. I felt terrible – as if I'd been caught out in the middle of a terrible crime.

'It's fine,' he said. 'I don't mind – not at all. You do what you want. No one else will see – unless you want them to, of course?'

I smiled at him. For a second I thought of putting my hand back where it was, straight away, just like that, so that he could watch me. I thought he could get onto his knees between my legs and stare at my cunt while I felt myself. He could lick me too if he wanted, or spank me, or tie me up and thrash me with his belt, or stuff a drink bottle into my anus. Oh yes, he could bend me forward over the table, tie my wrists with napkins and thrust the neck of a bottle into my anus. I could feel it now, stuffing me full. I could feel myself squirming on it. I felt my hand moving down. It was almost under my control – doing what I wanted – then something stopped me and I held back.

'Please, miss. It's fine. I don't mind at all.'

I allowed my hand to stray back between my legs. It was odd with him standing so close, just watching, but at the same time it felt so right, and so exciting.

I ran my fingers across the smooth material of my dress. I pressed them against the top of my crack – my clitoris was still hungry for attention. I probed down between the fleshy cleft and into the opening at its centre. The dress material made the shallow valley of my slit even more exciting – smoothing it out, enhancing its nakedness, tingling my flesh with the softest touch.

The young man watched me carefully, his eyes following the movements of my fingers, tracing the indentation they made of my slit, tracking the shallow groove the material picked out as it was pressed down against it. I increased the pressure on the material and lifted it slightly, revealing just the slightest glimpse of the flesh at the tops of my open thighs. His watching eyes filled me with excitement.

'Don't stop,' he said. 'Listen to the conversation. I will watch you all the time. I will hear what you hear, I will watch what you do, and I will be ready when you are.'

I did as he said. I listened to the two sisters, all the time feeling my cunt, pressing my fingers around my clitoris, watching the young man watching me, waiting until I would ask him to make my building pleasure complete.

'I'm embarrassed to meet you here like this,' said Vanya. 'It must be awful for you.'

'I don't mind. I know what it's like.'

'You're very kind, but it's worse than even you think. You don't know half of what he makes me do. He told me to meet you here today. Can you believe it? He said he wanted to know that I was sitting below the bedroom talking to you while he thrashed one of his girls. That's him now. Can you hear? Every one of those rhythmic smacks is him bringing his belt down across her upturned bottom. That's all he thinks of – thrashing girls, tying them up, stuffing their mouths – and always with me nearby. Sometimes I think I can't stand anymore.'

'Oh, Vanya, it must be so terrible for you.'

'It is, Jana. I have to wait here today until he comes down and tells me he's finished. He will bring her with him as well. She'll be hanging onto his arm as usual I expect, probably barely dressed. They'll sit down here and he'll then go on to tell me exactly what he's been doing. Jana! Can you imagine it?'

'I know what he's like. I really do.'

'I don't think so, Jana. You couldn't.'

'I do, I promise you I do. He probably never told you,' said Jana. 'He was giving me a lift home from college once. I was in the first year netball team. Look, I've still got the muscles!' She flexed her biceps in embarrassed fun. 'He said it wasn't out of his way. I didn't have time to shower or change – I was really sweaty! And my skirt and vest were still wet. It was a really hot day. Did he ever tell you?'

'No.'

'Well he drove me behind a factory somewhere. I was pretty excited – he was older than me, your husband, all that kind of stuff.'

'What happened?'

'He was very nice really to start with – considerate. He asked me if I wanted to kiss and I said yes. It was good. Then he said my clothes were very sweaty and I should take them off. I wasn't so sure about that but he was very convincing. He said it would freshen me up, that we could hang the clothes out of the window and they would dry and feel nicer when I put them on again. Well, I wasn't sure but I did anyway. I sat beside him in the car completely naked. I didn't really know what to do. I remember I pressed my hands together and pushed them between my legs. We kissed again. It was strange feeling his hands on my naked body. I can still feel it now. Wow! It was really exciting! Sorry, sorry, Vanya. I shouldn't have said that. But it was!'

'It's okay. I know he can be very exciting. It's okay. Just tell it as it happened. I won't mind what you say. Just tell me.'

'Well, we kissed some more – I told you that – and it felt really good, right somehow. Then he started to feel between my legs. No one had ever done that before so it was a bit weird, but it felt good. He pressed his finger into the cleft at the top of my cunt. I didn't know how to respond really. I opened my legs when he asked me and I moaned a bit because I couldn't stop myself, but it was all so new. I was more nervous than anything else.'

'I suppose he said he wanted to thrash you, or spank you?'

'Well he didn't say much, and he certainly didn't ask me, no. He sort of changed once he'd felt my cunt. He slipped his finger inside and pushed it up and down. He wasn't so nice any more – he felt crueller.'

'What did he do?'

'He took me by surprise. Everything changed. He dragged me out of the car. It had been raining and everything was wet. The next thing I knew I was bent over the hood, completely naked. He didn't give me any time to think. He bound my wrists with my knickers – you know, those blue ones we used to wear for games. He pulled them so tight, then he pressed me face forward against the cold wet metal of the hood. He pulled my ankles out and bound each of them to the ends of the front bumper of the car. He pulled my wrists together and found some rope to tie them with, then he wound that into the roof rack. I was so stretched out I could hardly breathe. Do you remember that roof rack?'

'Yes, yes. Go on.'

'I know there were some people watching, several men at least and a woman I think – workers in one of the factories. He took his belt off and strapped me across the bottom. I cried like anything – sobbed and sobbed, but he took no notice. He wouldn't stop. It went on for ages. I even think some of the men that were watching came over and took part. I can't remember properly. I know there were different shadows behind me. All I can really remember was sobbing like anything and feeling the never ending pain across my bottom. It was terrible – so fierce, so forceful, so biting. Vanya, it hurt so much!'

Jana slumped back in her chair. It was as if reliving the ordeal had brought it back too close. She wiped tears from her eyes. Vanya leant across the table and held her hand.

I realised I was still feeling my cunt, and that the young waiter was still watching, but now he was on his knees between my legs, his face only inches away from my slit, staring at my fingers as they felt the wet flesh and pressed against the tingling base of my hard and beating clitoris.

I listened to the thrashing going on in the room above the courtyard. The tempo was increasing; the slapping of leather against skin was becoming more intense – louder, faster, harder. The young man's face got closer to my cunt. The sister's voices became more filled with purpose.

'He got up on the hood of the car. He told me he would like to stuff my mouth with my panties but that he just couldn't resist putting his cock in there. He said I should never tell you. Yes, I remember now! He said I should never tell you about this, and that I should never tell you he had put his cock in my mouth. Well I never did, but it never happened anyway. He got it out. He held it in front of my face – it was really big, it looked heavy, I couldn't imagine how it would go in. But it didn't. I tasted it against my lips as he pressed it against them. I felt it beating and throbbing. I saw the veins sticking out along its length as I stared down towards its base but, as he forced my mouth wide with it, there was a sudden commotion. I'm not sure what it was – perhaps an argument with the other men that had come over, something disturbed him anyway. The next thing I knew I was being untied, lifted off the hood and put in the back of his car still naked and shaking like a leaf. He threw my clothes in after me and I got dressed as he drove me home. He reminded me not to say anything to you as I got out. He never spoke to me about it afterwards and I have never mentioned it until now.'

Vanya sat back in her chair and smiled.

'That was a shame for him, don't you think? That he should have been frustrated like that?'

'What do you mean? I was pretty frustrated myself. Oh, Vanya, I'm sorry, but I was.'

'Yes, I can tell. Perhaps there's a way of getting rid of the frustration for both of you. It's terrible that both of you are unfulfilled, don't you think?'

She smiled at Jana.

'Maybe.'

'Perhaps we should help him bring things to a conclusion at last. I hate to think of him not getting what he wanted. And things would feel better for you as well?'

'Maybe? Yes, maybe?'

'And I think I know how we could help him.'

She took Jana's hand.

'How?' asked Jana, as Vanya pulled them close together across the table.

I couldn't hear what they were saying – I could only stare at them – complicit creatures hatching a plan.

Suddenly, I was awakened to everything else that was going on – it was as if I had been asleep, in a trance or somehow transported to another planet. The first thing I sensed was the sound of slapping – leather against skin. It came back into my mind like a train approaching out of a tunnel – it hit me with the same blast of air and rush of sound. My head rolled from side to side with the shock of it. I could not hear her any more. I could picture him behind her though, she must be tied – and tightly too – and gagged. She could not be standing such a beating in silence without being gagged, and he would not be able to strike her so rhythmically if she was not held in place, unable to move, or squirm out of his range. I held my breath in expectation of the crescendo of his effort – the final stroke that would send her into unconsciousness, that would make his semen flow, that would cut the last stripe into her already red laced bottom.

Then I looked down and saw the young man between my knees. His face was pressed between the tops of my thighs, his mouth against the flesh of my cunt, his nose penetrating the crack, his tongue deep inside the opening. He was sucking and slurping at me, biting at my clitoris and at the flesh that surrounded it. I was pushing myself at him – giving him as much as possible, opening myself up to his feeding as much as I possibly could.

I felt the slurping frenzy of his hunger in my cunt. I heard the whirling passion of the beating in my head. I saw the conspiracy of the women and felt the waves of excited anticipation their intrigue brought with it. I was completely satiated. I felt myself in the grip of a constant orgasm, but I could not tell whether it was coming or passing, building to something more, or subsiding and leaving me used and depleted.

I could not choose any one thing over another – I was inundated with it all, drowned and wallowing beneath the frothing confusion that surrounded me like a churning whirlpool.

The next thing I knew the beating stopped suddenly – as if the strap had broken, or the woman had collapsed under the strain of her suffering, it was abruptly concluded. I imagined her licking his cock, sucking up the copious semen as it flowed over her hungry tongue. I imagined him throwing her clothes over her and ordering her to dress and go. I imagined her lifting her bottom so that the final few drips of semen could dribble over her burning skin and ameliorate some of the unrelenting heat and pain that she knew would last for days.

With the young man still slurping at my cunt, I saw the man and woman appear in the courtyard. She was tall and slender – truly beautiful. She hung onto his arm as he walked towards the two seated women. She had not done up her skirt properly and I could see the top of her left thigh and a hint of her panties between the edges of the open pleat. He wore faded jeans and had not properly buckled up his black leather belt. I knew that was what he must have been beating the woman with – she could not take her eyes from it. It was as if it was her master and she was watching for its further orders.

'Hello, ladies. Have you had a good concert? Did I leave the window open wide enough? I hope you didn't miss anything. My friend has been very eager to please. Look, her wrists are red from the binding I used to keep her from squirming, and her ankles too, where I had to tie her to the bed legs to stop her moving out of my range. She will not speak. Her mouth is too sore from the gag – it was large and has strained her. And it took a long time before it was over. She has had to suffer a lot for my pleasure.'

Vanya nodded graciously.

'Perhaps you are still not satisfied, my dear? Perhaps you hanker after some unfulfilled pleasure?'

'I feel like that,' said Jana. 'Unsatisfied. As though once something was started but never finished.'

'Yes, Jana has been telling me a story, my dear. A story about the past, when she was younger and was promised some satisfaction by a man but never received it. Perhaps you had a similar experience?'

The man raised his eyebrows and looked from one sister to the other.

'Perhaps? Yes, perhaps.'

'Yes, Jana, has been telling me the story in detail. It sounds such a shame to leave things like that, don't you think, even though it was some years ago.'

'Yes, it is.'

'Then perhaps we can bring it to a conclusion at last – right here, right now.'

The man looked uncertain, suspicious, but Vanya smiled and Jana reached out her hand to him.

'Yes, that would be very nice,' he said.

'Perhaps your friend would help us?'

He nodded to her. She let go of his arm and stepped forward.

Jana started taking of her clothing – her shirt first, then her bra, then her skirt. She stood in her panties and shoes as Vanya explained.

'Here, perhaps your friend will bind her. I think that's how she said it was. Yes, here, bind this scarf tightly around my sister's wrists. Good. Good. Now my sister will lie across this table, it's not like the hood of a car but it will serve the purpose. Do you remember now? Is it all coming back now?'

Jana leant forward, pressing her perfectly formed breasts against the smooth shiny top of the aluminium table. She bent at the hips, her bottom held up, her thighs taut and straight.

'Yes, I'm sure that will do, don't you think, my dear? Yes, I thought you would agree. Now perhaps your friend would help you bring out your cock. That is what we want isn't it, that is what you disappointed my younger sister with all those years ago. That is what you promised and never gave, isn't it?'

The man smiled as the woman encircled his hips with her hands and removed the belt from his jeans. She undid the button at the top and pulled down the zip. She grabbed his cock and brought it out in her hand – it was hard and throbbing, heavy and swollen with heat and excitement.

'Perhaps you will enjoy bringing the belt down across my sister's buttocks as you offer her what she has been waiting for all this time. Perhaps at last you will satisfy her with the pleasure and pain that has been withheld for far too long?

He took the belt in his hand as Vanya pulled Jana's panties down to her ankles.

'Now at last you will make it happen.'

The woman held the shaft of his cock tightly in her hand as she moved its end towards Jana's waiting lips. The man pulled the belt back and held it high, ready for the moment when it would be right to bring it down across Jana's waiting, exposed bottom.

Jana opened her mouth some more. I saw the flash of her teeth – they were white, beautiful. She opened her mouth wider. Her canine teeth were long and pointed. She turned back to her sister and smiled. Their tips glinted like diamonds in the morning sun.

'The problem is,' said Vanya. 'Things have changed over the years since you abandoned my sister. She is no longer the innocent girl you knew then. Look she has grown some new teeth as well. Her appetite is different these days, but she is no less hungry. And now she feeds until she has been completely nourished. These days she never lets go until she had taken her fill.'

Jana opened her mouth as wide as it would go. The woman fed the man's cock into it. Jana clasped her teeth around its shaft and bit down hard.

I rose up as my body was seized with a cramping paroxysm of overwhelming pleasure. I didn't know where it was coming from, where it would lead to. I thought I heard the belt being brought down but only once or maybe twice. I heard a scream but it was quickly stifled, and I heard slurping and greedy feeding but I couldn't tell whether it was coming from Jana's feasting or the hungry feeding of the young waiter as he buried his face deeper into the soft open flesh of my wet and dissipated cunt.

The young waiter brought me a drink and placed it in front of me on a paper napkin. I was shaking all over. I looked at my hands – I couldn't keep them still. I had hardly realised he had gone! My lips were dry, my mouth was gaping. My legs were still spread wide, my dress pulled up exposing my cunt. The insides of my thighs were wet with my own moisture and the young man's spit. For a moment I did nothing, then suddenly, as if caught by a cramp, I pulled my dress hem down and drew my legs together. My face flushed red. The young man left without saying anything.

Just as I put the glass to my lips two hands reached from behind me and clasped across my eyes. I choked in the glass and held it away from me in the hope it would not spill. It spilled.

'Surpise! Surprise!'

It was Sparky!

She released her grip, ran around and dropped to her knees at my side. She was wearing loose shorts and a white T shirt but with the same pink socks and white plimsolls she had been wearing before.

'I've changed! Look, Syra! It's a new Sparky. I found them in a laundry basket. What do you think?'

She jumped up and twirled around in a pirouette.

'You look nice, very nice, Sparky.'

'I'm so pleased you like it. I couldn't find any knickers.' She lifted the loose fitting legs of her shorts. 'See! And I've had a good shower. I feel so keen, so full of beans! Oh, Syra! I can't wait to get on with our investigation. Where shall we start? I know. We'll go to the club, the "Club Lichvář". That'll be the perfect place to sniff out the trail of the passport desperado! Let's catch a tram! I just love trams, don't you? Oh, Syra, I'm so excited!'

11. SPARKY'S DILEMMA

We waited at the main tram terminus – a huge circuit of tram lines festooned with wires on wooden posts and girdled by a glass covered waiting area supported by blue iron stanchions. Small red trams with white painted tops and wide open roof lights to let out the heat clattered around the circuit to the sound of ringing bells, snapping rail points and the constant fizz of sparking electricity.

Sparky jumped up onto the first one that stopped and dragged me behind her.

'Have we got a plan?' she asked excitedly.

'I just want to get my passport back. That's the plan.'

'Right-ho captain!' she said bringing her hand up in a brisk salute. 'That's what we'll do. The game's afoot!'

We got thrown off the tram a long way before our destination – we had not purchased a ticket and the non-uniformed conductor was not prepared to sell us one. Sparky grabbed the man's hand and pushed it down her shorts but it only seemed to make him angry. She tweaked his cheek with her finger and thumb, grabbed my hand and pulled me off at the next stop. She said it was just one of the problems of being an investigator.

As we walked along the narrow street to the club I could see that Anicka was waiting by the door. She was clearly jealous of Sparky leaving her and following me. She nodded coldly. Sparky ran up to her, wrapped her arms around her neck and kissed her fully on the mouth.

She pulled back breathlessly.

'Look, Anicka, I've got a new friend, Syra!'

'I thought I was your best friend,' said Anicka scowling.

'Well you are, well you were, well, it's different for Syra and me. We're on a mission, you see, a secret mission to recover something very secret. We are like conspirators so we need to be best friends. Syra's lost her...no, I mustn't say, it's far too secret...but we've come here to get it back, this secret thing, to track down the thief and have him locked up in a dungeon for taking it...the secret thing, that I mustn't say about.'

She gasped for breath.

Anicka scowled at me. I smiled but she looked away angrily.

'Why don't you stay with me, Sparky? There's a big crowd expected tonight. We could make lots of money. You know the mistress expects her commission. Come on Sparky. We'll get into terrible trouble if we don't work.'

Sparky pressed her finger to her nose in feigned thought.

'I don't think so, Anicka. Our mission is too important. You will have to do without me tonight. The mistress will have to wait for her percentage.'

Anicka turned away from her and leant against the wall, picking at it with her long finger nails as she kicked absently at a large canvas bag that lay on the ground at her feet. I saw tears in her eyes. One of them ran down her cheek and dripped off her chin.

It took me a few minutes to get used to the light inside the club. It was noisy and packed with people – scantily dressed young women danced frantically, eager young men attended them with pawing hands and longing stares. A young woman dressed only in shiny pink panties and matching bra was tied by the wrists to a rope that hung from a hook high above a small stage. A man at the side of the stage was winding the rope up on a pulley. Her body stretched up as the rope slowly tightened and brought her up onto her toes. Her taut slender body spun slowly as finally her feet came off the ground.

A small crowd gathered around her. Two women – one with short blonde hair, the other with slicked down black hair – stood at the front each with a man behind them. Both the men entwined the women with their arms, the one pinching at the woman's nipples inside her thin dress, the other running his hand up beneath her short skirt and pressing his fingers against her crack.

A man, dressed in a dark suit, shirt and tie, and carrying a briefcase, came onto the stage. He placed the briefcase down alongside the spinning woman. The black haired women at the front of the crowd squealed with enthusiasm. She grabbed hold of the hands of the man who was behind her and encouraged him to apply more pressure to her nipples. Her eyes widened with pleasure as he pinched them harder.

The man on the stage walked around the woman, looking at her carefully, checking her, poking her. He spun her slowly, ran his hands along the sides of her narrow waist and up between her taut thighs. He took hold of the waistband of her panties at the back. She stopped spinning. He pulled them down to behind her knees then set her spinning again. He opened the briefcase and laid the two halves flat. Inside was a curled up leather whip with a heavily braided handle. He removed it, still wound up, then flung it out to its full length across the stage. The woman tied up by the rope looked fearfully at the extended whip each time she turned and it was brought into her view. The man snapped it back. It cracked loudly and its end gave off a spark as it accelerated and burned hot.

The blonde woman at the front of the stage stretched back and wrapped her hands around the neck of the man behind her. He pressed his fingers harder against her cunt, pulling them along the slit, lifting her short dress and exposing her glistening naked flesh. The black haired woman pressed forward against the pinching fingers around her nipples, increasing still more the pressure, the pain and the delight that came with it.

The man on stage took back the whip. It curled in the air. He snapped it and brought it forward. The loud crack made me shiver. Sparky grabbed my hand.

'Syra, come on! We need to get on with our mission!'

The whip went back again, this time curling in a lazy loop as he flung his hand forward and aimed it at the hanging woman. The tip pursued the line he had set it. It flew past his head and, coinciding with her slow rotation, it touched the woman's bottom before snapping back with a sparking crack as he drew his hand up again and prepared it for the next.

The woman screamed. She tensed her body but she had nothing to purchase against – she was like a fish dangling on a hook, able only to flex and wriggle, able only to demonstrate fear and terror.

'Syra! Come on!' urged Sparky.

The man brought the whip forward again. Its slow curl seemed to take an age but, by the time it reached the point at which it must snap back for its return journey, it perfectly matched the position of the woman's naked bottom. She was completely exposed to it – unable to protect herself or move away, unable to cower before it, unable to avoid its pain. And she could not beg for mercy, or plead for forgiveness for a crime she did not understand – the pain was too great. The combination of the deep cutting pain and the burning sting were more than she could put into words, she was only able to let it out in the only sound she could make – a breathless, howling screech.

Again it came down. The black haired woman in the crowd fell forward to her knees. The man behind her lifted her dress and plunged his finger into her anus. The whip came down again, the suspended woman howled in pain. I smelled the burning of leather as it cracked against her skin.

'Syra! Come on!'

Sparky pulled insistently at my hand. I felt myself moving, being drawn away, but my eyes were still fixed on the hanging woman, my senses still inflamed by the sight of her suffering, my needs increasingly to witness it all, to watch it until the end.

Sparky pulled me away. She dragged me through a door and into a room filled with boxes. Clothes of every description and colour spilled from their open lids. Sparky rummaged in one of them and pulled out a short black jacket with gold buttons and a shiny gold skirt. She held them up against her.

'What do you think? Good?'

I nodded, confused by her random attitude, still thinking of the woman on the stage, still hearing the cracking whip, still smelling the smoke from its sparking end, still shivering from the howling pitch of her penetrating scream.

Sparky took off her shorts and T shirt and pulled on the gold skirt. It fitted her perfectly. Her breasts were small and pert and I delighted in seeing their delectable tension as she pulled on the tight black velvet jacket and buttoned it up. She reached into another box, pulled out a magician's joke plastic flower, attached it to the lapel of her jacket and ran to the door.

'Come on! Come on!'

I ran after her. We went down a short corridor. It was hard to see – only a flickering single light bulb lit the way. An old piano was pushed amongst some curtains. It was covered in dust. Sparky ran up to it, flipped up the lid and placed her hands on the keys.

'Look!' she shouted excitedly as she ran her fingers up and down randomly. 'Sparky and her tragic piano!'

I was panting for breath as we stopped by a door at the end of the corridor. It was slightly ajar. A yellow light drifted like a sallow mist out of the open crack at its edge. I could still hear the screaming woman, but now only faintly. Yes, I could still hear burning crack of the whip followed by the piercing screech of agony. Just knowing the woman's punishment was still continuing released a thrill that ran right through my body. I shivered.

We peered into the room through the crack. My mouth gaped wide. In one corner a young woman stood naked with her panties pulled down around one leg. In the centre of the room a naked girl with a sponge bound to her mouth with string crawled on all fours. She bent and mopped up water used to clean the floor with the sponge, crawled over to a bucket and squeezed the sponge out before returning to the task of mopping up more water. The air was heavy and hot – moistened by the water on the floor and heated by a noisily spluttering gas fire, it was sticky and humid. Pastor Wick sat in a leather chair behind a desk in the corner opposite the standing girl. He held a Bible in his hands.

Sparky pulled at my arm.

'Syra! Look on the desk. Some passports! Do you think one of them is yours? Syra! It's so exciting! Our mission! Our mission!'

I looked at the passports on the desk. They were spread out. One of them was certainly the right colour. Yes, it must be mine!

Pastor Wick started reading from the Bible.

'This is my lesson to you, taken from Exodus, Chapter 1, verse 11: "So they put slave masters over them to oppress them with forced labour'. And as the Egyptians oppressed the Israelites, so I bring you to obedience. I teach you with the same hard hand. And likewise, I am both your king and your master. Oppression and ruthlessness are the watchwords of slavery; pain is the essential ingredient of obedience for only through pain does enslavement leads to faithfulness. What use are you as a slave unless you are completely obedient? Here, my little slave, as you work for me and mop the floor what do you think about? Yourself? Of course not, you think only of me, your master, and what it is I can bring you. Perhaps I will bring more suffering, or perhaps I will allow you some respite from your misery. Whatever, it is in my gift. And my other slave. You do not even know what choices I have planned for you. You wait, exposed and humiliated wondering only what it is I will bring to your life, what it is your destiny will be at my hand. Perhaps I will thrash you, or make you suck men's cocks for sixteen hours, or throw you into the streets, or send you to collect blood for me. Ah, I see the thought of blood brightens your eyes. Would you like that to be your future, little one? I could send you with a bucket and you could collect as much as you like. But it would still have to be warm when you returned with it, and I fear you would not be quick enough and you would return it cold. No, I will not inform you of your fate yet. You must wait a while until I decide. Your greatest fear for the moment will be that you do not know what is ahead for you.'

He turned suddenly, as if he had heard us breathing.

We both froze. My heart was beating loudly in my chest. I felt sure he would hear it. I wanted to clasp my hands over it, to muffle its sound, but I didn't dare move.

He looked towards the door and stared hard at it. For a moment, I thought he could see us. I felt as if he was looking right through the door and seeing us crouching fearfully behind it, like schoolgirls caught smoking, or meeting boys, or swapping homework. I felt shamed by his penetrating stare.

He turned away. I breathed again and squeezed Sparky's hand. She squeezed back and lifted her shoulders in barely suppressible excitement.

'And the LORD said; "I have heard them cry out to be rescued from their slave drivers"! Do you cry out to be rescued my little slaves? Do you wish to be saved from the delightful oppression of slavery?'

He dropped down on his knees beside the woman mopping the floor with the sponge.

'Do you wish to be rescued? Are you unable to suffer more? Do you want to be returned to your former life?'

The woman shook her head in panic, fearful that he might reject her, frightened that she might be taken from the suffering that he imposed. I could see she was already lost to him – to his control, to the delights of his punishment. I could see that her life was pointless unless she was his captive.

'I will pray for you both. I will pray that, when the time is right, you can perform the tasks you are set and can meet with my approval.'

He got up and turned to the wall. He held the Bible in his hand, closed his eyes and began praying.

Sparky grabbed my arm tightly.

'Now's our chance. Syra, we can get it. He won't see us. I know he won't. Syra! Come on!'

I held back. It seemed too risky. How could we know how long he would be distracted by his prayers? And what if he heard us? What then? And the women? They would see us. Surely they would shout to him, let him know!'

Sparky pushed the door open. The woman with her panties down around one leg looked over immediately! Surely she would cry out!

Sparky opened the door some more. She pushed herself into the gap and sidled into the room. She looked back, expecting me to be behind her. I was still hiding behind the door.

'Syra! Come on! Come on!'

'Sparky, I can't. I just can't.'

She hesitated for a moment – unsure what to do – then she smiled and turned back.

'It's okay. I'll do it, Syra. Sparky's on the job! Sparky will complete the mission!'

I could hardly bear watching her. I bit my lips and felt my heart racing. I was breathing hard – gasping, struggling to get enough air. My hands were shaking. I felt consumed by anxiety.

Sparky crept across the room towards the desk. The woman in the corner watched her all the way. Sparky half smiled at her but seemed uncertain about her response. The woman with the sponge in her mouth carried on working. Sparky brushed against her. The woman looked up. Her face was filled with fear. Sparky moved towards the desk.

She was so close to Pastor Wick! Surely, if he did not hear her he would smell her, or sense the unsettledness of the two women he had enslaved?

Sparky reached the desk. She picked amongst the passports. She looked inside one and held it up. I could hardly bear it!

'It's yours!' she mouthed silently. 'Yours!'

I waved to her to come back, but she carried on looking on the desk. I could hear her shuffling amongst the passports. Surely Pastor Wick would hear her too. She picked up another and looked inside. She dropped her head from side to side as she looked at it quizzically. I waved to her again to come back. She held it up and waved it from side to side excitedly.

'Syra! It's me!' she mouthed. 'Me!'

She jumped up and down, unable to contain herself.

I could tell she was going to speak. I could see she was finding it impossible to contain her voice, to keep quiet about her discovery. I put my finger across my lips and urged her to keep silent. I wanted to see her rush back to the door. I wanted to grab hold of her hand and for us both to make our escape. She opened her mouth. I nodded my head at her, tapping my finger on my pursed lips, urging her desperately to stay quiet and come back.

'Syra, it's me!' she blurted out. 'Me! It's a passport for me as well, but it has a different name, it's – '

Pastor Wick swung around immediately. His prayer broken and confronted by an intruder, his face filled immediately with rage. He threw the Bible down and grabbed Sparky's arm. He spun her around and grabbed the passport from her hand.

He looked around. I could tell he was looking for me.

'Where is she?' he shouted at Sparky. He pushed his face in front of hers. Her eyes filled with tears. 'Where is she? Does she think she can trick me? Does she think she can steal her passport from me and escape? And you! You look so puzzled at your discovery. Why do you think you are here? Why do you think the mistress pays you? Did you think it was out of generosity? You foolish child! This is your new identity. You are on the list to be sent to America to start your new life. Your new master has already paid for you.' He grabbed the passport and thrust it in front of her face. 'This is you now. Look! Soon you will start your new life – with your new name!'

'It's not true! It's not true. I'm Sparky. I'm Syra's friend. You will – '

'It is just as well that you have come here. You can stay now. A little training with my two little slaves here will help you be more obedient. We can't have your new owner disappointed now can we?'

Sparky struggled to escape. He was far too strong for her. He kicked out at the woman on the floor. She fell to the side, still clasping the wet sponge in her mouth. She tried to get back on all fours again but again he kicked her and she fell back. The other woman did not move. I couldn't tell whether she was frozen with fear at Pastor Wick's rage, or whether it was her commitment to carrying out his instructions to wait that kept her in place. The scene was bizarre. I felt myself pushing at the door and as I did I realised I would never enter the room.

I moved back from the door, aware that Sparky was struggling against Pastor Wick, aware that my fear was overtaking me and that I was preparing to abandon her. I knew I should rush in and help. I knew I should be faithful to this innocent elfin creature who had made herself my friend, but I was too afraid. But my passport! For a moment I stopped and turned. But no, the urge to run was too powerful!

'Run, Syra! Run!' shouted Sparky. 'Don't worry about me. The mission. Think of the mission!'

Pastor Wick realised where I was. He let go of Sparky and ran towards the door. Sparky grabbed his leg and sunk her teeth into his calf. He turned and looked at her, fixing his jaw and breathing hard through his nostrils to stifle the pain. She looked up at him, narrowed her eyes, and bit even harder. He raised his hand, preparing to bring it down on her. Everything seemed to stop – as if it was waiting for me to make my decision. I ran.

I heard his hand make contact. I heard the breath knocked from her as it did. I could to tell where it struck her, but I felt the pain as if it was my own as I dashed away and left her behind in his grasp and at his mercy.

I ran back along the corridor and into the club. Again the sound of the whipped woman filled my head. It was as if it had been held back, saved up, and now it all flooded out in a dam bursting rush. She was still hanging on the ropes. Her bottom was covered in burn marks from the tip of the cracking whip. Angry red lines striped her hips and her back. Spit ran from her mouth in a continuous stream. Her body was not so tense now; it had slumped on her wrists, hanging loosely on her bonds, no longer able to tense when the whip struck her, hardly able to allow her enough breath to cry out in pain when it did.

The black haired woman in the audience was lying on her front with her head turned to the side. She had been stripped naked. She was surrounded by men, their cocks in their hands. Semen ran from her mouth. Her back, her buttocks and the backs of her thighs and calves were covered in it. Her hair was sticky with it. It oozed from the crack between her buttocks. Her eyes were wide and vacuous – she looked totally depleted and used.

The other woman, the blonde haired one, knelt by her side, her breasts exposed, her nipples red and marked by pinching. She held her hand underneath the other woman's face, cradling it, helping her to take more semen as it flowed down from the men's cocks above her. The blonde haired woman turned towards me. She opened her mouth; I though perhaps she was going to shout, to encourage others to pursue me, to hold me prisoner for Pastor Wick, but she did not. She stretched her lips wide and showed me her teeth. It was enough, and she knew it, just to let me know that her pointed canine teeth would soon be puncturing her friend's neck and she would be feeding from her greedily until she was satisfied.

I was in a nest of vampires and I didn't know what to do. All I could think of was escape. All I could feel was blind panic.

I ran out into the alley. Anicka was still standing by the wall. She stepped out and barred my way.

'Do you want your box back?'

I didn't know what to say.

'Didn't you realise it was us that stole it?'

'No,' I said unable to stop my voice from shaking.

'You can have it back if you want. I didn't want it anyway. It was Sparky who wanted to take it. She liked it because it was shiny. You can have it back. Here.'

She pulled the box out of the canvas bag at her feet. Its plastic surface glinted in the flashing neon light that hung above the door. I felt vomit coming into my throat. I grabbed the box and ran away as fast as I could.

12. THE RACECOURSE

I don't know what time it was when I finally got back to the hotel – it was beginning to get light. I fell asleep within minutes and didn't wake until late that night. I sat on the edge of the bed in the darkness trying to work out what was going on.

I'd lost the only person I knew here. And I'd abandoned her! I couldn't believe how I had left her there! I felt terrible. I wondered what was happening to her. I couldn't bear to think about it. I felt so guilty. And the chance I had for getting my passport back seemed to have gone completely. Surely I wouldn't be able to trade the box with Pastor Wick now! How could I think such a thing? And why was there another passport for Sparky? What did she mean; it was her but in a different name? And why so many passports anyway? What were they all for? Who were they all for? What had Pastor Wick meant abut going to America as a slave? I couldn't understand that at all. My head reeled with questions but my mind was a blank with any answers. I felt hopeless, stupid and lonely, and cried as I went to sleep, my finger stuffed in my cunt, slowly trying to ease my pain.

The next morning things felt no better – I was still racked with guilt, still worried about Sparky, and my mind still teamed with unanswered questions. I walked around Hlavné Námestie Square feeling doomed and lost. I wanted to eat but my money had nearly run out, and I had no way of paying the hotel bill. I sat on the edge of the Maximilian Fountain dipping my fingers in the clear rippling water. I looked at the reflection of the sky in the moving broken water. It resembled the confusion of my life – fractured shapes drifting apart, nothing firm to get hold of, everything in permanent disarray – I felt like sobbing.

I don't know why – I just felt compelled – but suddenly I turned and looked across the square towards the white and pink painted buildings on the other side. I saw a beautiful woman in a red dress walking assertively between the café chairs and tables spread out over the pavements. My stomach immediately filled with anxiety. I recognised her straight away. It was Miranda!

My first thought was to run over to her, to grab her, to ask her for help, but I stopped myself; something held me back – a suspicion, a sense of dread. The same force that had compelled me to look up somehow stopped me from approaching her. I thought of our last meeting on the plane. She had been so friendly and so passionate, but there was something about her that made me feel uncomfortable, somehow suspicious.

I stared at her as she strode to a tram stop. Why was she here? Surely this couldn't just be a coincidence? Then I remembered what the man from Acme Couriers had said about being visited by an FBI agent in a red dress! Of course, that's where I had first seen her – coming out of the Acme Couriers office in the airport! And now she was here! Not just in Bratislava but in Hlavné Námestie Square, where I was!

I dodged behind the central pillar of the fountain. Emperor Maximilian stood over me in full armour – the town's protector. I looked up at him and prayed that some of his protection would spill over onto me. A flurry of wind blew up and some of the spray from the fountain flew up and drenched me. I felt as if I had been baptized, made safe, somehow given a new sense of purpose amidst the confusion that was threatening to destroy me.

I stepped out from behind the fountain. My dress was wet at the front. It clung between my legs – revealing the crack of my cunt, sticking to my breasts, exposing the prominent hardness of my nipples.

Miranda got onto a tram. Just as its bell clanked and it began to move I jumped up behind her. I don't know how she didn't see me! I walked straight past where she was sitting, looking to the opposite side, holding my hand up against my face. I walked to the back and sat down. My heart was pounding. I couldn't believe it! I was filled with apprehension but I was also burning with excitement! Perhaps I had truly been baptized!

The red and white tram crossed the huge "Pristavný most" bridge over the Danube. It was teaming with pedestrians and cyclists and, on either side of the roadway, passenger and goods trains struggled to enter or exit the city. After clattering for a while along the edge of the river a huge park area opened up. Most of the passengers got off at the same stop, Miranda amongst them. I waited until she was walking along the pavement before I jumped off. I could see where we were heading – Bratislava's hippodrome, the horse-racing track. Large banner signs on the side of the road told me where I was – "Petrzalka" – a haven of peace on south side of the Danube, in a crook of a long bend, opposite to the main city. It was a fantastic mixture of greens. Trees grew everywhere – some isolated, some in copses, some in woody knots – and the racecourse wound its way between them like a muddy green river. People around me chattered eagerly, many in English. I heard straight away what was going on – it was the height of the racing season, mid-June, and one of the most popular Sundays of the year with more than twenty races scheduled for the day. Everything was buzzing with excitement and anticipation.

I followed Miranda into a steeply banked stadium built alongside the finishing line. The whole place was full of colour – blue, red, gold, silver. Everyone was dressed up; everyone looked perfect – at their best. A fluttering confetti of betting slips thickened about their feet as ever more promised winners came to the post unplaced.

Suddenly, she moved on. It was hard to keep her in my sight as she weaved amongst the thronging crowds. She made her way to the parade ring, circuited it, then went into a small brick built tack room.

Inside a man was waiting to meet her. They shook hands and kissed. Miranda sat down on a low bench with a rounded seat covered in shiny leather. The man stood in front of her.

I squeezed behind a huge weighing scale. I could hear everything they said.

'How many have you got for me this time, Miranda?'

'Ten. All beauties. You wouldn't believe some of them. So naive! I've had a couple working for me at the club for months now. They're so stupid. One of them is called Sparky! So scatterbrained! Anyway, yes, ten. Have we got clients for them all?'

'Every one of them, and paid for handsomely. There's never a shortage of takers. It seems as though every wealthy American wants a Slovakian slave.'

'The more the merrier. Now, we have the new passports ready – Pastor Wick has organised that. But he's been getting some trouble from a woman acting as a courier for Acme. We can't afford to lose them – we'd never get other couriers as good as them to move the girls across the Atlantic. And we need the money – Pacific Heights could not operate without it. So we need to sort things out a bit. This little troublemaker is important to the flock, *very* important. We need to get her on the next flight out. The shipment leaves tomorrow anyway. But she's got the box and she hasn't handed it over. She's no idea how important it is. I think it was a stupid idea to send it this way, but the Acme people said that using an innocent always makes sense. The trouble is that this "innocent" also happens to be someone we really need. Pastor Wick should never have let her slip away from him in San Francisco. Then, by sheer chance, she walks into Acme Couriers! It's a good job I was there.'

'Do we know where she is?'

'Yes. I've been keeping my eye on her ever since we left San Francisco. Pastor Wick says he'll go to her hotel later tonight, about midnight, and get the box. He'll be in the club until then. A bit of last minute training with a couple of the girls, he says. He's never satisfied until they are perfect! Anyway, yes, he will pick up the box and bring her as well, whether she wants to go or not! He says that as far as her use to the flock is concerned she doesn't have to be willing anyway. He says he will just drug her and transport her back. He will probably keep her like that, he thinks. It does not matter whether she is conscious or not, he says, as long as the flock can feed on her. It is a nice thought – the flock sucking up their nourishment while she sleeps, don't you think?'

'So, for now, we've got a bit of time.'

'A bit, yes.'

'Do you have still any instructions to carry out?'

'Yes, I have one more before carrying out my final instruction. It is the reason I suggested that we meet here.'

'Perhaps you should use it now.'

'You make it sound like the last of my three wishes!'

'Well, it's a bit like that isn't it?'

She nodded. My heart quickened as I remembered what had gone on in the restrooms at the airport at San Francisco.

Miranda pushed her hand into a small leather purse slung from her shoulder.

She pulled out some money.

'Dollars alright?'

He nodded, took the money and counted it carefully.

She was doing it again, following the same routine that I had witnessed before – paying someone to provide a service that had been prescribed by her absent master. Yes! That's exactly what was happening! I brought my shaking hands together between my legs. I pressed the backs of them against the insides of my thighs and forced them apart enough to feel the coolness of air against the naked exposed flesh of my cunt.

I pulled myself down behind the huge "Toledo" weighing scale. It was massively built – a big circular dial at the top, a heavy green painted frame, and a shiny metal platform on which the jockeys stood to be weighed. By the side of it was a chair and just beyond that a rack of riding crops, all of different lengths and materials, some with coloured tips, some with differently braided handles, all with loops to wrap around the rider's wrist. Beyond the rack of crops was the leather covered bench on which Miranda was sitting.

The metal of the weighing scale was cold to the touch. I pressed my cheek against it and breathed in deeply as it cooled my skin.

Miranda stood up, turned around and held her arms above her head. She said nothing. The man took hold of the hem of her red dress at the back and lifted it up. She had a tight black lacy thong pulled between the crevice of her buttocks. He drew the dress above her narrow waist and up along the full length of her arms. She was not wearing a bra and I just caught sight of her breasts springing back tightly as the waist of the dress pulled them upwards and released them as he dragged it higher. She stood perfectly still as he drew it up over her hands. She waited for a few moments after he had tossed it down on the floor – still and silent – before finally lowering her arms and allowing them to rest at her sides.

I tried to imagine what her instructions were. She obviously knew them perfectly. She must have memorized them all. She must know which ones she had completed and which were left outstanding. I wondered what form they took, whether they were written down or whether her master had forced her to recite them until she was word perfect. Yes, I decided that must be it. He had bound her to a chair and left her in a small dark room, visiting her every few hours to rehearse her in his instructions. He would stand over her as she repeated them back to him. When he brought the session to a conclusion he would gag her and draw a hood over her head so that there were no distractions as her efforts continued until again he returned. If when he tested her she made a mistake, he would release her from the chair and tie her down across its seat so that he could cane her or whip her. Perhaps sometimes he would spank her or use his belt, I could not decide. Yes, that must have been how she had been trained to such a level of obedience. And now she was at her last but one instruction – carrying it out as if it was her first; devoted to the detail of it, bound by its perfect achievement, committed to its precision.

Miranda turned sideways to the leather covered bench, lifted her one leg over to the other side of it, lowered herself forward, pressed her face against the smooth black leather, and rested the flats of her palms on the floor on either side. Her breasts and stomach were pressed against the leather cushion, her bottom rose up in a delectable curve with the lacy black panties outlining them at the top as their narrow waistband ran off at right angles down onto her silky skinned and shapely hips.

I drew my hands from between my thighs and smoothed them along the upright length of the heavy frame of the weighing scale. Its even metallic surface was a delight – cool, lifeless, unresponsive, brutal; a delightful contrast to the warm responsiveness of my own skin. I wanted to lick its hard exterior, run my tongue along its unyielding shell – taste it, smell it, feel myself at one with it. I wanted to experience the interface between the living and the lifeless – the animate and the inanimate. I wanted to feel the bond between that which knew, and that which knew not.

The man ran his hand along the dipping curve of Miranda's back. She rose slightly against it, pressing back against the pressure of it, responding to it, showing him how sensitive she was to it. It was her first and only signal.

He let his fingers rest on her buttocks. He pressed at them, testing their elasticity, their suppleness. They responded by first giving to the pressure he applied but straightaway returning to their original firm form as soon as he pulled back. A small white imprint, where his fingertip had been, faded quickly – like a puff of mist on a summer's morning it dissipated leaving only a dewy remembrance of its fleeting presence.

Suddenly, he turned and walked out of the low roofed brick room.

I stared at her as she remained, still motionless and silent straddling the bench. I waited, my heart pounding, my mouth open, my tongue reaching out towards the cool metal of the weighing scale's heavy frame.

I wondered how long I would have to wait, and for what? I couldn't imagine what was going to happen. I opened my legs wider and pressed my crack against the sharp edge of the weighing scale's heavy back. Again I felt its coolness, its hardness, its rigidity. The dial was like a massive head, the glass covered front its face, its massive chassis its muscular body. I imagined it as a strange lifeless god – the god of the dead, set on the shores of a sterile planet to guard against the infection of the living. I pictured myself before it – fearful in its presence, shaking with fear at my closeness to its daunting power.

I stared at the line Miranda's black panties described around her hips. I imagined how tightly the narrow gusset was between the crack of her buttocks. I imagined the material stretched across her anus and pulled in between the fleshy edges of her cunt. I pictured her covered slit pressed against the leather cushion of the bench – moist, hot, waiting for ecstasy, for fulfilment, for completion. I pictured it moving against the material of her panties, the material moving against the leather. I thought of her flesh, all the time separated from the leather, anxious to get in contact with it, needing it and yet revelling in the movement and silky contact that kept it apart. I thrilled at the images of those shiny surfaces moving together against each other – the tension, the delectability, the promise.

A door was opened at the other end of the claustrophobic, low roofed building. A shaft of brightness broke in, highlighting the brick walls in its light – red, loosely mortared, dirty and damp. For a moment, I imagined I was inside a huge empty vein. Someone entered. It was not the man who had left. This man was smaller, slimmer, brightly dressed. It was a jockey.

He walked in carrying his brown leather saddle, worn to a shine by years of racing and training. He wore a helmet with a blue silk covering. His silky shirt was a matching blue with large white diamonds front and back. The shirt was pulled tightly at his neck where a white collar was clipped. His white jodhpurs ended just inside the red tops of his shiny black leather boots. He went to the rack of crops and selected one, testing its tautness and weight by slapping it against his hand and the side of his jodhpurs.

Miranda did not move at all, even though she must have heard the jockey behind her. She remained in place straddling the bench.

I pressed my cunt harder against the sharp edge of the weighing scale chassis. I stepped forward and let my foot rest on its patterned steel platform. The finger of its gauge moved slightly around the face as it detected the pressure of my foot. I no longer cared if my presence was discovered – I was too close to the metal god to fear the eyes of mortals.

The jockey did not hesitate, he did not assess the situation, he went straight up to Miranda and laid the brown leather saddle across her back. It fit perfectly into the curved dip prescribed by her spine. He pulled the front cinch strap tightly beneath the bench and secured the saddle on her back. Still she did not move, or show any response to what was happening.

I wrapped my arms around the weighing machine and pressed my foot harder on the platform. The finger moved again around the dial. I thought for a moment it was a blinking eye – that the machine had come alive, that I had roused the god from his slumber, that he was responding to my touch, encouraging me to get closer, tempting me to rub myself harder against his monolithic frame.

The jockey pulled up the cinch strap into a D ring. Miranda was pinioned onto the bench, pulled down by the tensioned strap with the pressure and weight of the saddle clasped firmly against her back.

The rear of the saddle lay above the waistband of her thong leaving her bottom exposed and unprotected by the material that was pulled in between the crack of her buttocks.

The jockey mounted her as he would his horse – jumping up athletically, lightly and with an agility born of experience and practice. He drew up his knees and inserted his feet into the high stirrups. He fixed them in place and dropped his body slightly forward. He gripped his riding crop in his right hand and rose up on the stirrups.

Still Miranda did not move. I knew she was having to tense herself to take the strain. I knew she must be struggling for breath. I knew she must feel frightened at the confinement of the binding that secured her to the bench. I knew that she must be apprehensive of what was happening and what was about to happen. But also I knew that she was carrying out her instructions, instructions issued by her master, committed to memory and now at last brought to life by their enactment. What greater pleasure could there be than to carry out her master's orders in such a way? He was not even there to witness it! That made it perfect – a silent homage of subservience, like a prayer to a great god, a sacrifice to the one who was above her in every way.

I moved more onto the platform of the weighing scale. I felt as if I was standing before my master – like Miranda, knowing his silent orders, about to carry them out without his knowledge or intervention. I was in the presence of perfection – carrying out the perfect deed of submission.

The jockey started riding her, his buttocks off the saddle, his knees bent, his head forward, his crop held firmly above her exposed bottom. He flexed his legs – raising and lowering himself at a pace, urging himself on, rounding the last bend, looking for the finishing straight and the final gallop to the post. His breath was fast and regular. The crop came down repeatedly. It smacked sharply and quickly on Miranda's bottom. It was a snap, so quick it could hardly be noticed, always in movement, always punishing, always ready to punish. He rode on, his breathing quickening, his eagerness increasing, his need for speed escalating.

I reached up to the dial of the weighing machine. It looked down on me – benign and unthinking. Yes, it was my master. I opened my legs to him, exposing my fleshy cunt to the ungiving metal of his body. I held my hands up and embraced the neck of the dial. I looked into the face of my master – my true god. I didn't need to ask instruction; I knew what I must do. How could it be otherwise?

The jockey's pace quickened, his breathing became more rapid, the crop came down again and again. The snap of contact – leather against skin – was harsh. Miranda did not react to it; the resilience of her buttocks soaked it up. I looked at her face, to see if she was straining to stand the pressure of the jockey on her back. Her mouth was open, a slight trickle of spit was running from the corner of her lips, but there was no sign of anguish or distress, only a fixed stare that spoke of her sense of purpose and dedication to her master's wishes. She was doing everything she could to carry out her instructions perfectly, everything she could to fulfil the wishes of her rider and the punishing ferocity of the lashing whip.

I pressed myself against the lifeless body of my master. His coldness and ignorance of me fed my delight – it was his very distance and lack of concern that drove me forward into his ungiving arms. I pulled the front of my crack against his body. There was nothing to bear against – no knob, no protrusion, no handle, nothing to slip into the notch of my flesh. My frustration was overpowering. He would not offer me anything – just obedience and effort, just my own suffering as I tried desperately to carry out his demands.

The flat folded end of the crop snapped again and again – always harder, its resonance longer lasting, the pain it inflicted never ending. The jockey's breathing became more intense, his movements more hasty. The crop struck harder still. I could see in his mind that he had rounded the last bend, that he had seen the final straight. The cheers of the crowd were filling his head. He brought the crop down again and again in a frenzy – he was thrashing her wildly now, demanding the last effort from her, riding her to the point of destruction.

I looked at her body, still unmoving, still simply suffering, simply carrying out her instructions, every moment of her own silence bringing her increased pleasure, every second of unresponsiveness setting off delights inside her like no action ever could. I looked at her face. The trickle of spit had lengthened; it was bubbling now, frothing and leaching out over the leather cover of the bench. There, at last, in its glistening strands, I could see the fullness of her pleasure. I could see in its trickling, bubbling stream her unreleased bliss, her imprisoned ecstasy. Her orgasm would not flow, he had not instructed her to release that – that was part of his instruction – but he had not told her that she should not anticipate it. He had told her that she should not have the joy of knowing its rapture – the fulfilment of it by its escape into the world – but he had not told her she could not imagine all that it might be, that she could not experience the delights of wanting but not having.

Suddenly, I caught her eye. She looked straight at me. She had known I was there all the time. I felt the incredible pressure of her pent up pleasure. Somehow she passed it to me and I was filled with it.

It broke over me like the waters from a bursting dam – I was drowned by it. I clung to the body of the scales – the form of my master, my god – barely able to hold on, barely able to stay conscious as I listened to the continuously smacking crop and the urgent breathing of the still frantically riding jockey.

I didn't know how long it went on – my head buzzed and I felt giddy as it ran through me. I jerked and shook. I think I screamed out, but I was not sure. All the time Miranda stared at me, all the time the spit ran from her mouth, all the time she made no sound and did not move, all the time she was in the ecstasy of anticipation.

In the end I fell sideways from the platform of the scales. It was like being tossed from the knees of my master as he threw me aside – unwanted, used, and now dispensable. I dropped on the floor, still shaking and jerking from the pleasure that had run through me like a scorching fire. I clasped my fingers against the flesh of my cunt. I could feel it throbbing, beating with the delight of abiding by my master's silent wishes. I delved them deeply, feeling the wet flesh around them, lubricating them, making their passage easy, drawing them in, letting them become a part of the pulsating delight that was gripping me in uncontrollable waves.

I looked at Miranda again. Spit was still running from her mouth in a stream. The jockey unbuckled his saddle and began walking out of the room just as another came in. The second jockey went up to the rack and selected a crop, testing it as the first jockey had done by flexing it against his hand and smacking it against the side of his jodhpurs. Satisfied, he stood forward ready to take his turn with the captive who would suffer punishment until her instructions had expired and who throughout it all would not be satisfied because the instructions she followed so meticulously prohibited it. I looked at the rack of riding crops and realised that Miranda would have many more riders until her penultimate task was brought to its conclusion.

I almost crawled from the weighing room – I was completely dissipated. I made my way back to the hotel in a tram, thinking all the time of what I must do now that I knew what was happening around me. I needed to clear my mind, to decide on a course of action and to follow it without hesitation. I knew I didn't have much time. Miranda had said that Pastor Wick would be visiting me late tonight. Yes, I knew what I must do. I needed to rescue Sparky. I couldn't live with myself knowing that I had abandoned her to the cruelty of Pastor Wick. And now I knew she was going to be exported as a slave, my mission to save her was unquestionable.

13. THE BOX IS OPENED

I didn't stay in the hotel room for more than a few minutes – just long enough to grab the box and get out.

I rushed down the stairs and straight out into the street. It must have looked as if I wasn't coming back because the girl at the reception ran after me waving a piece of paper.

'Miss Baund! Miss Baund! You cannot check out! Miss Baund! You have not paid.'

I took no notice, swerved into the main square, and quickly lost her in the crowds.

I knew now that Pastor Wick not only wanted the box, he wanted me! And he was prepared to take me in any way that suited him. I wasn't going to let that happen. And I wasn't prepared to allow him to take Sparky – to sell her into slavery just to help finance his evil pursuits at Pacific Heights. I'd get her out and we would both escape and that would be the end of it – Pacific Heights and all that went with it would be forgotten at last.

Everything seemed frantic as I rushed through the streets. I felt desperate now – to get my passport, to make it up to Sparky by setting her free, to escape, to wake up from this terrible nightmare. The world around me seemed in turmoil – the sprawling chairs and tables on the pavements seemed like an infection, a virus that was spreading over the city, consuming it and burying it beneath its monstrous contagion. I tripped over the leg of a chair and the box went flying. A young woman picked it up. As I saw her carrying it towards me – as I realised it was separate from me – I was overcome with anxiety. The thought of losing it now was more than I could bear. As she got closer I became more panicky – her long strides, her fixed stare, her never ending approach all contributed to my feeling of helplessness and threat. I grabbed it from her and ran without even saying thanks.

Soon I was running down the alley towards "Club Lichvář". It was dark now and the flashing neon light cast a multicoloured pool of light around the entrance door. I shivered as I saw it again.

Anicka stood by the door pulling on her panties. She glowered at me as she bent her right leg outwards at the knee, held the gusset in her fingers and spread it out across her cunt. I could see she had been crying. Her nipples were hard and prominent beneath her thin gold lamé top. She brushed herself down nervously and walked over.

'I thought you were leaving. I gave you your box. Why haven't you gone? If you go then Sparky will be my friend again.'

'Sparky has been taken prisoner. I have come back to help her.'

'And take her away, I suppose.'

'You are both in danger. Don't you realise that?'

'Why don't you just take the box and go! Leave me and Sparky like we were before you came.'

'Anicka, you are both in danger!'

She looked so forlorn. I wasn't going to convince her, I knew that. I pushed past her. She looked surprised and frightened. She called after me, her voice cracked and desperate.

'Don't take Sparky away from me! Please don't take her away from me! She is all I have. The only friend I have! I don't think I can live without Sparky! Please, please don't take her away! Please!'

I burst into the main club room and was hit by the noise and heat. Suddenly, I realised I didn't know where to go – what to do! I looked around; everyone was gathered around the stage. A woman was bent over the back of another on all fours. She was being beaten and the crowd were encouraging a man with a whip to strike harder, to bring it down faster, to make her suffer more. As the whipping continued, she screamed and writhed so much she had to be held in place by several other men. Every time the whip came down the crowd cheered and bayed for more.

Above the dance floor, and spanning two sides of the cavernous room, there was a raised gallery edged with chrome banisters and with open metal flooring. Different coloured flashing lights in transparent tubes hung around it in twisted loops. It looked like a spaceship, or part of a city from a distant planet. A figure leant over the banister watching the woman being beaten on the stage. Each time she screamed out he smiled – gratified by her suffering, pleased by the enthusiasm of the crowd, ennobled by his position of power over them all. It was Pastor Wick! I had found him!

I didn't think, I just ran across the room and up the open metal stairway onto the balcony. I watched him all the time, fixing him with my eyes, afraid I might lose him. But my stare did not keep in place. By the time I reached the balcony he had disappeared through a heavy green door. I just saw it closing behind him as I reached it.

If I hesitated it was only for moment – not even long enough to make me stop. I lunged at the door, grabbed the handle and rushed straight in, not thinking of what I might find, or how I would deal with whatever it was.

As if I had suddenly appeared from nowhere, I found myself standing in a small room holding the box in my hand. I gasped for breath as my heart pounded wildly in my chest. As suddenly as I had appeared in the room, a tide of fear came over me. It consumed me in a massive drowning wave. I tried to inhale but it was impossible.

I fought for air. I felt giddy and sick. I looked around, trying to stop the dizziness, trying to stop myself from fainting. I gulped hard. The room was cluttered with furniture – things piled up on top of others. The lights were dim and yellow. It was so hot! A spluttering gas fire was full on and tall French windows leading onto a balcony were tightly closed.

Sparky, wearing only her pink panties, was bound tightly to a chair, her head hung forward, her spiky hair adorning her like a surreal crown of thorns.

She looked up at me. A leather strap was tied across her mouth – she couldn't speak. She widened her eyes and nodded excitedly. Blood trickled from two puncture holes in her neck. It had run down over her small breasts and stained her pink panties. I wanted to go to her and lick it up, to clean the wounds with my tongue – to taste her blood. Yes, I wanted to taste her blood! Suddenly, that was all I could think of. I wanted to suck in her blood and drink it. I wanted to feel it going down my throat, being absorbed into my body, becoming part of me.

I shook my shoulders, trying to rid myself of the images that were filling my mind. The lust for blood had taken me over so quickly. It seemed to come from nowhere. The idea of its sudden appearance frightened me. I felt so out of control. I bit my lips and held my breath – trying to force myself to think of other things. My heart was bursting! I clenched my fists and pinched my nails into the palms of my hands. The pain helped. I dug them in more. I felt the skin breaking, the blood flowing. But the sensation of my own bleeding started it again. My mind filled with images of redness, of nourishment, of drinking blood. I stamped my foot on the ground, like a child in a temper, trying to assert myself over unruly thoughts, trying to regain control. I kept telling myself why I was here – why I had compelled myself to come to this place. "I am here for my passport. I am here to help Sparky", I repeated in my mind as I struggled to blot out the images of blood, the lust that was coursing through my veins, and my need to feed on it.

Pastor Wick's voice broke my reverie. It was like being woken from a deep sleep – like being yanked back into a world that had seemed lost.

'Ah, Syra, I see the sight of blood inflames you. The germ in you cannot be resisted. Can you smell it? Can you already taste it on your lips? Here, come closer. Put your lips against her delicate neck. Lick out your tongue; touch the fragrance that calls us all to the source. Here, Syra, come and drink at the well of life. Your little elf is waiting to give you her essence. Here, sup at the wounds that I have made for you, drink from them they are not yet healed.'

I felt myself stepping forward. Everything he said made sense. Yes, I wanted to drink from her – *needed* to drink from her. Nothing else mattered. I walked closer to Sparky. It was as if I was in a trance. Her eyes widened even more. She nodded her head, as if trying to tell me something. Her excitement was overflowing, boiling out of her. She was frantic. I raised my eyebrows, to show her I didn't understand, but really all I was thinking about was the wounds in her neck and the blood that was still flowing from them. All I could think she was trying to say was "Drink from me! Drink from me!".

I didn't notice him taking hold of the box – I had completely forgotten I had it! I watched him slipping it from my grasp, but its loss meant nothing to me. All I could think of was Sparky's neck, the taste of blood and my need to feed on it – to drink it, to have it within me, to know her completely through it.

Suddenly, he pushed me forward. I stumbled and fell. He drove his knee into my back, pulled my arms behind me and tied them tightly together. It all happened in a second. The next thing I knew he was dragging me over to the bed. He threw me down and lashed my ankles together. I rolled onto my side unable to get up. I twisted and writhed – filled with panic, terrorised by my sudden captivity, horrified by the way I had lost control of myself.

It was pointless trying to free myself. I lay on my side, my heart pounding and gasping for breath. I watched Sparky still animated and excited, still nodding her head, still trying to tell me something that still I didn't understand.

Pastor Wick stroked my forehead.

'Oh, Syra, this could have been so much easier for you. You know we must have you back – the flock is nothing without you. But you don't have to go willingly. Your agreement is irrelevant. The next thing you know you will be there again, in Pacific Heights. In fact you may not even know that. I may keep you sedated so that the flock can feed without hindrance. You don't need to be conscious to be of service. Just think of it, Syra. Think how marvellous it will be. They will come to you daily; they will wait patiently for their turn to feed. They will use the same wounds I expect, although some of them will sometimes want to start afresh. Your neck is the best place, but some will want to use the insides of your thighs, or under your arms – all good places to draw your special blood. And you will know nothing of it. Syra! Don't you find that so exciting? You will sleep through it all.'

The thought made me shiver – my blood ran cold with the thought of it. I squirmed against my bonds, but it was useless, they were far too tight.

He ran his hands down my neck and onto my breasts. He encircled them and pinched my nipples through the thin material that covered them. He slid his hands down the front of my stomach and down between the tops of my thighs. He squeezed his fingers against my cunt. The material of my dress was folded over his hand and the movement of it against my flesh sent a rush of excitement through me. I shivered again, but this time not in fear but with exhilaration. He lifted the hem of my dress and looked at my slit – I had no panties on. He pressed my knees wide and held them apart. I tried to push them together – not knowing why – but he was strong and it was impossible anyway.

'That is such a sweet slit,' he said running his fingers along the soft crack.

I felt the harshness of his nails against the sensitive folds and, because he was no longer holding my knees apart, and even though I knew I didn't want to, I quickly brought my legs together.

'That was a mistake, Syra,' he said angrily.

He reached back and held up some thin leather laces. I stared at their potential and my stomach filled with anxiety. He wound one around my left knee and stretched it over to one of the legs of the bed. He pulled it tight, yanking my knee down against the bed before tying it off. He did the same with my right knee. I was spread out completely. I felt so exposed, so prone, so open. My slit was splayed wide, the glistening valley of flesh at its centre so open and bare. I wriggled against my bonds and could turn my shoulders from one side to the other, but my hips and legs were firmly fixed by the tightly pulled laces.

He stretched out his fingertips and ran his long nails along the exposed flesh. It sent shivers through my hips and, when I struggled to move and realised I could not, the shivers intensified. He did it again. The thrilling shivers ran into my anus. I felt it dilating. I couldn't stop it. I squeezed my buttocks together and the sensation only deepened.

'Before you go to sleep, you might appreciate help with your dreams. Yes, if your life is to be only dreams, let them be drawn from memories which gave you pleasure. And not only memories of past events but memories of what you wished for, what you anticipated. And aren't the best things, Syra, those expectations, those yearnings, those hopes? Think how it feels right now, Syra. Are you wondering what will happen? Are you thinking of the things I might bring to you? Are you anticipating the joys that might come? Are you imagining that beautiful thought that will stay in your mind forever? Of course you are. And they are the root of your pleasure. Imagine this state fixed in your mind, Syra, forever there, forever in your dreams. Imagine, Syra, dreaming forever.'

He grabbed the arms of the chair Sparky was bound to. He dragged it closer to the bed. He grasped her by the hair and held her face so that she was looking straight at me.

'Your little friend can watch. Perhaps she will enjoy the show? Yes, I can see she is already excited by the prospect! And when you dream your eternal dream you will be able to see her face forever looking at you, enjoying you, wanting you.'

Sparky's eyes were wide. I stared at her pink panties pulled so tightly against her cunt. She looked so fresh and delightful. She shook her head from side to side, trying to free herself, trying to throw the strap from her mouth. She was seized with desire, filled with purpose. I could only think she wanted to free herself so that she could bury her head between my legs, suck at my cunt, lick it, and probe it with her tongue.

Pastor Wick unbuckled his brown leather belt. He drew it out of the loops at the waistband and wound it around his hand. Its brass, heart shaped buckle twinkled as it picked up reflections of light from the spluttering gas fire. It was as if the belt itself had flames at its end – a blazing heart ready to burn itself into my very soul. The image scorched itself into my mind.

He opened his hand and let it unfurl. It was long and broad. Its hard glossy edges shone like strips of light. Its shaped end, forked and with serrated holes for the pin, was like the tongue of a venomous snake. I pictured it flicking out at me – threatening me with its poison, terrorising me with its potential for my destruction.

I realised my mouth was open – gaping, hanging loosely as if I had been put into a trance. I tried to close it and realised I couldn't; I had lost control, my terror had taken me over.

He stood back and smiled. It was that look of arrogance, of mastery over me, which finally overwhelmed me. With that one arrogant grin my fear, already making me shake with terror, turned to an uncontrollable panic that dissolved everything I could hang onto into an ungraspable fluid of dread. Everything that had happened to me had led me here, everything that I had tried to achieve had failed, and now I was tied out like a captured beast before my tormentor, exposed and waiting for his punishment, entirely at his mercy, my destiny at his whim. And there would be no end to it. He planned a life of sleep for me, a life where my blood would service the ends of others but of which I would be unaware. The horror of it all descended over me like a dark poisonous cloud. I was buried beneath it, choking on it, my lungs stuffed with the awfulness of it all, my mind filled with revulsion and despair.

He was careful to aim the belt so that it landed precisely at right angles across the slit of my cunt. The picture of it coming down was terrifying but when it struck, the impact, the penetrating pain, the dragging of my flesh, the burning, the shock of it all was so great that I screamed louder than I could ever have believed possible. He held back on the second, watching my contorted face, seeing my twitching uncontrolled body, witnessing my twisting hips and squirming shoulders. When he had seen enough, he took aim again. I didn't know if I could stand it, and yet I didn't know what failing to stand it meant. Would I pass out? Is that what he wanted? Would this punishment itself be the sedative that would drive me into the lifelong unconsciousness he had planned?

The leather belt fell again on its target. It pulled sideways at the flesh of my cunt. I howled. It was so heavy. Its smacking sound filled my head. The next time it came down, I couldn't hear anything – I was screeching before it even landed.

I thought of looking over to Sparky but I couldn't lift my head. Another smack came down, another howl, followed by another and yet another screech of pain. Some of the blows struck my anus – I felt it dilate then contract. Some of them struck the backs of my outspread thighs, some the insides of my knees, but always in the end he returned to my cunt, always he found his aim again across the slit of my most sensitive flesh. And when he did I was totally consumed by the pain it inflicted – everything else was driven from my mind.

I opened my eyes and stared up at him. I thought of it as my last sight. I imagined capturing the image of him in my mind forever; knowing my punisher, seeing his face burned into my brain for eternity.

He pulled the belt back. I could not tense again, any resistance or reaction I had was now gone. He held it there. I waited, expecting this to be my final image. But he did not bring it down. I waited and still nothing happened. He struggled, as if fighting with himself, as if his body was unable to carry out his brain's instructions.

He twisted and turned. A shadow was about him – a dark creature on his back! I thought it was a devil, an evil presence come to commend me to hell. The shape clawed at his face, I saw its hands covering his eyes, its fingers grasping the corners of his mouth. A flurry of bright red hair appeared behind his head. It was not a devil clawing against his back. It was Anicka!

I was still jerking with pain as I watched her wrestle him to the ground. He fell sideways under the combined weight of her body and the frenzy of her attack. She was manic – her face filled with purpose and anger, her limbs, agile and wild as she pounded him with her fists, clawed at him with her finger nails, bit into his ears with her gnashing teeth, and kicked at him with the pointed toes of her wrinkled leather boots.

He dropped heavily to the floor, his head banged hard against the gas fire. He was limp and unconscious by the time his arms had settled loosely by his side. A spurting flame erupted from the fire as if to testify to her victory.

Anicka crawled away from him, like a tide-washed crab, she scuttled to Sparky and dragged the leather strap from her mouth.

Spit flew from Sparky's mouth.

'Syra! Syra! Look at my panties! Do you like them? They are pink like before. Do you like the way they cover my cunt so tightly? Syra! Syra! It's so exciting!'

She couldn't keep still as Anicka released her. Straightaway, she rushed over and began helping me free. I dropped back still with my legs apart. Sparky dropped her face between them, splaying her open mouth across my flesh, filled it with her tongue and covered it with her spit. My fear and pain was immediately replaced with an overwhelming feeling of delight. It was as if angels had suddenly transported me from the bowels of hell and dropped me into paradise. I was being licked by an angel, pampered by a heavenly elf whose only concern was my happiness. I closed my knees around her head and squeezed her face as close as I could. I knew she couldn't breathe and I felt her holding her breath. I knew she would stay there until I was ready to release her.

She gasped when I let her go. She sat up straight on the edge of the bed and placed the flat palms of her hands against the sides of her face.

'Syra! I have had such a time! I was waiting for you. I knew you'd come. And you've brought Anicka with you – dear Anicka. Now we can all be best friends!'

She threw herself forward and again buried her face against my cunt. I felt her lapping at it, sucking at the flesh, biting at my clitoris. Anicka watched, stroking Sparky's back tenderly, happy again just to be with her and be counted as her friend.

Sparky drew back again breathlessly, kissed me on the mouth, sucked at my nipples one by one then jumped down and picked up the box which had fallen to the floor. She placed it next to some passports on the small table with the green baize top. She looked amongst them, retrieved one and held it up as a prize.

'Here you are, Syra! At last! The mission is complete! We have found your passport!'

I smiled at her – she looked so happy, so charming, so pleased.

'Yes, Sparky, the mission is complete.'

Excitedly, she picked up another two passports and looked quizzically at the pictures on them.

'Syra! Here is Anicka and me. But why do we have different names? Syra! Why do we have different names? I feel lost, Syra. I'm all mixed up. I feel as if I don't know who I am. What's happening, Syra. Tell me, please, what's happening? I am not me. Anicka is not Anicka. Syra, please help me, please!'

'Sparky, it's so – '

'Oh, Syra! It's so exciting! The mission is complete!'

I stared at the box. Sparky saw me and shared my gaze. Her eyes lit up. The box was at the centre of all that was going on. Suddenly, I was transfixed with it. In this room, with all the horror and fear, still with Pastor Wick lying on the floor, with Sparky and Anicka, and knowing we must get out – still with all these things I had to look inside!

I opened it! I just grabbed the clips on the side, undid them and flung it open!

The heart inside was wrapped in cling film. There had been ice around it, but it had been too long and now it was melted. The melt water flowed out as soon as the box was opened. The heart was more brown than red, its entire surface covered by the shiny cling film that helped it keep its shape. This was Father Dawson's heart – the very organ that kept his evil alive. I couldn't believe it! I took it out – it was heavy. I nodded to Sparky. She sat on her hands, hardly able to control her excitement – bobbing up and down, licking her lips, and jogging from side to side.

I unwrapped the heart carefully. It lost its shape as the covering came off. I held it in my hands – flaccid and wet, oozing blood, the arteries and veins that connected it now whitened and hard.

Anicka draped her arm around Sparky's shoulders as they both moved closer.

There was only one thing to do. I knew that I must consume it. I didn't feel apprehensive. There was no revulsion, no horror, I just needed to eat it.

I offered it to Sparky. She opened her mouth as it approached. I pushed it forward, knowing she shared my wish, that her only desire was to feed on it. She was infected by Pastor Wick. The heart would consolidate that infection – now she would know the taste of the original master. It touched her lips. The stale blood ran down her chin. She opened her mouth wide and began to tighten her jaw onto the muscular flesh. I leant forward. I couldn't hold back any longer – the yearning for it was running through me in huge waves. As she brought her teeth down into the heart so I did the same – biting into it as she did, holding it between us, kissing through it, eating the flesh of it, sucking up its brown blood, gnawing on its sinewy tissues, feeding on its evil.

Sweat rolled down my cheeks as we fed, its salt adding piquancy to our feast. I watched Sparky's eyes – bright, enlivened, full of vigour and energy. Our lips kept touching as we ate the heart. In the end we were only kissing – our mouths open, our tongues probing, our banquet complete, our appetites satiated.

Finally we lay back on the floor. Sparky's face was covered in blood, her legs were wide open, her pink panties still pulled tightly against her cunt. I leant over and licked along the gusset. I pulled it away at the edges and tasted her bare flesh – soft, delectable, sweet.

I listened to the gas fire spluttering as I licked her deeper. I felt so hot. I heard Pastor Wick moan – he must be coming to. I had forgotten he was even there. Suddenly there was a strange muffled bang. I felt the pressure of it against my skin – hot and forceful. I turned and saw huge yellow flames pouring from the front of the gas fire. The carpet was already alight.

I jumped up and stood by the French windows. Anicka was already on the balcony. Thinking only of escape I ran to her. The flames were now reaching around the chair that Sparky had been bound to

'Sparky! Sparky!' I called out. 'Quickly! We must get out!'

'The box! Syra! Your passport! Our mission!'

She stood on the other side of what now was a wall of flames. It was like a curtain between us. She had the box open and was pushing some paper or something into it. She seemed oblivious to the threat of the flames around her. Pastor Wick was by her side, struggling to his feet, holding his bleeding head. Sparky reached out to me, as if she suddenly realised she must try and escape, but the flames were already too fierce for her to break through and the curtain of flames drew together and parted us completely.

14. THE FIRE

The flames engulfed the building. Scantily clad and naked women ran in panic from the club entrance. Billowing clouds of smoke burst out with them as they fell to their knees coughing and choking.

One of the women – young and slender with flaming red hair, and bright red fingernails, and excited by the panic and terror the fire was causing – dragged a man on top of her. She tore open his trousers, grabbed his hard cock in her hands and pulled it into her open cunt. She pulled herself against it, thrusting on it, anxious to draw out its semen and still unsatisfied when she did. She was frantic. She pulled herself off his cock, fell to her knees and started sucking it. She drained it all, slobbering at it hungrily but making sure that none of it escaped. Even when it had all gone, she pulled at his cock with her firmly clenched fingers and sucked loudly in the hope of more.

I looked up to the balcony. Sparky was trying to squeeze through the windows that led out onto it; they must have slammed shut when Anicka and I made our escape. Sparky just managed to get through. It was tight and she cut her arm on the jagged edge of the rusty latch. A blob of dark red blood dribbled down onto her wrist. She was clutching the box close to her breasts. She waved – it was as if she was excited at seeing me by chance in the street. She came out onto the ledge. Smoke clung to her spiky hair and red sparks fell about her head. She was panting – gasping for breath. Suddenly, she looked afraid, filled with foreboding. I knew her heart must be pounding with fear; the veins in her neck must be throbbing and making her dizzy. She put the box between her feet and she leant onto the balcony rail. Her fingers slowly stretched open as she felt the heat of the metal. I watched the blood from the cut running down her arm – it was as if it was running to slake the heat of the hot iron against the palms of her hands. It flowed between her fingers as she clutched onto the searing balustrade. I imagined the blood steaming and it was heated up. I imagined the smell of it – acrid and salty, biting and pungent. The scent of it must have increased her panic. Yes, she must be inhaling her own steaming blood.

Unable to suppress happiness, she waved again. She smiled broadly. It was as if there was nothing else in her world except me. I smiled back. It seemed ridiculous. I held my hands up – reaching towards her, as if I was offering to catch her and save her. She smiled again and nodded her head. For a moment I thought she was going to jump. She was surrounded by a cloud of smoke then, as it blew away on an updraft of scorching air, she picked up the box and threw it down to my waiting hands. I caught it. She waved again. I think I called to her to jump or try and climb down, I'm not sure. She started to climb over the balustrade. I could see it was burning her, I could see her pain, but still she tried as hard as she could. She looked down into the darkness below. She looked pitiful, as though she realised that she did not know what was beneath her, that she was unbearably afraid of the empty void that she faced, the abyss of unknowing that was her future.

I shouted to her, screaming at the top of my voice.

'Sparky! Sparky! Try! Try hard!'

Suddenly, I saw her body jerk. I thought perhaps the heat of the metal on her hands was too much, that she could not stand it or was jumping back in fear of the dark emptiness beneath her burning feet. She jerked again and this time fell back onto the balcony. She still managed to hold on with her fingertips for a few moments.

I screamed to her to try and hang on, to try harder, to put up with the pain, that it would pass, that she could save herself if only she hung on. But I knew it was hopeless – in my heart I knew she was lost.

The smoke surrounded her. She was disappearing into it. I saw her jerk again and realised she was being pulled back! The smoke cleared for a second as a burst of flames spilled from between the balcony doors. There were hands around her ankles! Yes, she was being pulled back into the room!

Her arms strained out towards me, her fingers stretched and reaching, but she could not resist the pressure on her ankles. Unerringly, she was pulled backwards across the metal grill floor of the balcony and into the smoke and flames of the room.

I stood waiting for ages, mesmerized, hoping that she might suddenly emerge, that any moment she would wave and call down to me, but she did not. In the end, as the flames reached up to the high pitched roof and curled into the smoky sky, I knew she was lost.

It started to rain – suddenly and heavily. It brought the smoke down with it. My lungs were full of it. The wet cobbled street glistened around my feet. It was like standing in a shimmering hellish sea.

They brought Sparky out and laid her down in the rain, her bare back against the cold wet ground, her eyes staring blankly up into the downpour. The neon light above the entrance to the club still flashed, highlighting her face and hair in a macabre mask of redness. They laid Pastor Wick alongside her – the murderer and his victim, bound together in death.

I wanted to fall on my knees beside her, to wake her up, to bring her vital spark back into the world, but instead I stood, frozen with fear and remorse, unable to even to blink my eyelids.

Anicka took the place I wanted to inhabit. She knelt at Sparky's side, massaging her, stroking her, trying to bring her back to life. Her tears fell on Sparky's face, but they could not revitalise her, they were only a balm of sadness, a solemn wetness confirming the misery of her departure.

'Wake up, Sparky. Sparky, Wake up,' Anicka kept repeating, as though the invocation would work where her tears had failed, but even her incantation was insufficient to reverse the change from life into death. Her piety and devoted effort could not bring Sparky back to life.

A fire appliance drew up behind them. The shiny steel ladder of the fire engine began extending as the hose reels were pulled out from the sides. Within seconds water was spraying over the flames. Sizzling steam rose from it. Acrid choking smoke descended to the ground and swirled at my feet.

The red haired woman did not stop sucking hungrily at the man's cock. She squeezed it in her hands. She took it deep into her throat, pressing her lips against its base as she swallowed on it in the hope of drawing out still more of its nectar.

I dropped down and sat on the wet cobbles, now soaking with dirty soot stained water that streamed down the side of the burning building in a waterfall. I held the box across my knees. I gripped it tightly, knowing that it was at the heart of what had happened, and that it was Sparky's last gift. I pictured her again throwing it down to me. I saw how pleased she was that I had caught it. Her face had lit up when I had secured it in my grasp. And it seemed so strange. Why had she been so desperate to get it back to me, she knew the heart was no longer in it? Why had she been so pleased that she had seen it in my hands even though she must have known her own fate was by then sealed?

Water from the building splashed down onto me, and the rain continued to pour. I felt as if I was in a storm of fire. I looked down at the dirty water that had washed from the building mixing with the rain that was running around me. I was sitting in a pool of it. I felt it against my bottom. I felt sullied by it – dirty and degraded. The water was not cleansing me, it was contaminating me. Suddenly, I had an overpowering need to be punished. I wanted pain. I wanted to suffer at someone's hand. I wanted to be a victim, to feel that I had no control over my destiny. I wanted to be humiliated and disgraced.

I opened the box – I don't know why – and saw straightaway that my passport was inside it! That's what Sparky had been so frantically stuffing inside. That's what she had been saving from the flames. A rough note, scrawled in haste on a charred piece of paper with bright red lipstick was pushed between its pages. I could hardly bear to read it.

"Syra! I'm so excited! Here is your passport. We have achieved our mission! We are such good investigators! XXX."

I clutched it in my shaking hands and broke down in uncontrollable sobbing.

I listened to the spurting water as it sloshed over the hot burning building and splashed down onto me, covering my head, my shoulders, my legs and feet. I smelled steam; its moisture filled my nostrils. I looked again at the note. Already it was soaked, its words disappearing in drawn out runny strands of red. The kisses at its end now looked like bloody scratch marks etched by fingers from which the nails had been roughly pulled.

I stared out through my tear soaked eyes. The steel ladder was high above me. A fireman on the platform at its top was struggling to restrain the powerful hose as he directed it over the roof of the building and in through the French windows where I had seen Sparky dragged back by the clawing hands of Pastor Wick. At the base of the towering ladder the red haired woman who had been sucking the man's cock was pawing at three firemen who stood around her.

The firemen's yellow shiny waterproof trousers glistened wet in the flickering light of the fire. Their tan coloured braces, hung on their broad shoulders, pulling the loose waistbands of the heavy trousers high onto their muscular chests. The red haired woman's face was wet – I wasn't sure whether it was from spilled semen or water. Her dress was little more than a sling across her shoulders. She pulled it off as if she was dropping a handkerchief and it fell like a wet rag around her feet. She stood naked in front of them, her red hair blazing in the flickering light. She turned and leant against the side of the fire engine, holding her arms up high against its red painted side before pressing her naked body against the smooth glistening metal. She squirmed against it, rubbing her nipples and the notch at the front of her cunt hard against its surface. In her movements I saw her delight – the sensation of her skin pressed firmly against the smooth metal, her exposure, her need.

A narrow hose with a shiny brass end dangled from a metal cylinder above her head. One of the firemen reached up and yanked it hard. A length of the hose spun off the wildly rotating cylinder that held it. It curled around her like a snake, slapping her back and twisting about her feet. She pressed herself harder against the side of the red fire engine – the sensation of the slapping hose only increased her desire for contact with the smooth metal. Her hair blended against it and the light from the flickering of the flames seemed to set her on fire. She seemed to be burning like a passionate, out of control torch.

The firemen pulled her from the side of the fire engine. She fought against them, suddenly wanting to stay where she was, finding comfort in the contact she had with the smooth metal of the vehicle, the heat of fire on her back, and the unfulfilled potential of only imagining what might happen to her.

One of them sat on an aluminium step built into the side of the fire engine. The others pushed her face forward across his knees. It must have been the sudden contact with the shiny waterproof material – perhaps it was cold or hot, I didn't know – but she reared back, writhing against the firemen's controlling hands as if she was in pain. For a moment I saw her hard nipples. The sight of them filled my cunt with a wave of pleasure. I pushed my hand between my thighs – I couldn't stop myself. Water dripped from my elbows to my wrists. I watched it running down the back of my hand and dribbling between my legs. A thrill filled my stomach. I licked my lips and fixed my stare on the struggling woman.

One of the firemen forced his hands against her back and drove her down. As she fell forward, she reached her hands out across the cobbles and straightaway the other firemen stood on them, pinioning them fast, holding her in place. The sudden sensation of captivity filled her with a fresh fear. I could tell from her jerking movements that she was overcome with dread. I could see from her frenzy that the horror of her situation had dawned on her anew. She wriggled against them, trying to snatch her hands way from the heavy feet that held them down, struggling to push herself up against the hands pressing down on her back and pinioning her so tightly against the seated man's knees. All her efforts were hopeless – she was overpowered, pinioned, and completely under their control.

I held the palm of my hand against my naked cunt – pressing so flatly against it filled me with joy. I kept it there – feeling the fullness of my flesh. I didn't want to move it for ages – the heat, the wetness, the way my legs were splayed apart, the feeling of proneness, all conspired to fill me with pleasure. The fireman holding his hands against the woman's back released her but she did not rear back or try to get free, she lay still, so dominated that she now no longer needed physical restraint. I drove my fingers into the crack of my cunt and at the same time pressed myself down heavily against them. I gulped noisily as I felt myself stuffed. I wanted my whole hand inside. I wanted to be filled with it, plugged by it. I wanted to feel that instead of it being in me, it was me who was draped over it. I swallowed hard and drove it in until I felt my wrist against the dilated flesh at its entrance. My mouth gaped wide.

The fireman behind the red haired woman took the brass hose end and held it over her buttocks. It glinted in the flickering red light of the fire. I thought she would move, that she would come to her senses, struggle again to release herself – but she did nothing. Perhaps she thought they would free her now, perhaps she did not realise that anything else was planned for her, that her destiny was already prescribed by others, perhaps she knew there was no longer any point in trying to summon up the will to act – it was impossible to tell.

I pulled my hand in and out of my cunt – that was all I could do to even partially satisfy myself. I watched the fireman pulling the trigger of the brass hose end – it was slow, considered, premeditated. I waited for the drenching spray. I wondered how forceful it would be, whether it would be a trickle or a deluge, whether it would bring the suffering of stinging pain or the gentle sensation of delicate joy.

I pushed myself back against the wall so that I could push my hand in harder. At last the trigger was fully pulled in. The spray issued from its end. It was a deluge

– a forceful flood of water that streamed out with such force it knocked the red haired woman forwards against the man's knees. There was nothing gentle or delicate about it – it was fierce, punishing, and hurtful.

I knew I was plunging my hand in and out of my cunt – I could feel it, I was filled with the joy of it, the terrible plugging of it – but all I could see was the powerful spray of water splashing on the woman's back. It was like a flood of blood – shimmering red in the blazing flames, covering her body in a sparkling scarlet torrent, smearing her crimson. It mixed with her red hair, ran off her face, dripped down her outstretched arms and onto her pinioned hands.

I knew I was crawling forward, on my hands and knees across the wet dirty cobbles. I hadn't got my hand inside my cunt any more – I could tell that – but I felt wetness across it as I brought my knees forward and squeezed each of its stretched edges tightly against the other. I was lured by the crimson spray. All I could see was its redness, all I could smell was the steamy moisture of it, all I could feel was its heat as it drew me forward crawling on the soaking dirty cobbles.

I clung onto the fireman's leg as he pushed the nozzle of the hose into the red haired woman's cunt. He injected the spray into her. It flooded out and ran down her legs in pouring streams. She must have tightened against it – she could not have done otherwise. She screamed, I think, but my head was buzzing so loudly I couldn't be sure. It rained from her, as powerful as when it entered. I crawled beneath the forceful plume, allowed myself to be covered in it. I offered my buttocks to it, my cunt. I wanted it in me as well. I wanted to be consumed by it. I knelt before it, waiting for it, longing for it.

When it came into me I screamed. It was everything I wanted – a spray of crimson rain, filling me full, drenching me from the inside, I revelled in it as it filled me. I absorbed all of it as I knelt on all fours in the splashing pool it formed around me. I don't know how long they kept it in – I felt so giddy and confused. I was thrashed with the hose for a while, but I only remember things clearly again when the spray was driven into my anus. As I was consumed by again by the delectable flood in my rectum I began to feel my orgasm overtaking me. It came in spasms to start with, but soon it joined together into a wave so strong, so sustained, that I lost myself to it, falling into an unknown place where only the delights of joy existed and I did not.

I sank my teeth into the red haired woman's neck, I remember that, and sucked at her blood as the water streamed into my rectum. I sucked so hard, I guzzled so greedily, that I thought I would drown myself in it. I didn't know if I was swallowing it or breathing it. All I know was that I was filled by it, drenched by it, and covered in it as I drank from her at the same time that I was filled with the red flaming spray beneath the blazing light of the still burning fire. All I felt were my jerking seizures, my captivity, my soaking and the fire within. All I know was that in the end I didn't know the end. When the flames of the fire burned away, when the blood was spilling from my mouth in sloppy globs, and when the spray from the hose, the drenching rain and the cascading sparks from the fire blended together, the red turned to darkness and I gave myself up to the shadows of a complete and fulfilling pleasure such as I had never even imagined possible.

15. MIRANDA'S LAST TASK

I sat in the airport, my head in my hands. I didn't know why I'd come here. I didn't even know how I'd got here. I didn't have any way of buying a ticket either. It was ridiculous. I realised I was here only because I didn't know what else to do. I felt stupid and hopeless.

The box sat heavily on my knees. It had brought so much trouble, so much suffering. I wanted to throw it away. I thought of abandoning it. I looked into the main concourse. A tall elegant woman in a red dress was striding towards me. It was Miranda!

I sat frozen to the spot. I didn't know if I was even thinking anything – I felt numb all over.

She stood in front of me, looking down on me. Anicka stood just behind her staring at the floor and absently kicking her heels.

'We are together again, Syra. I'm so pleased to see you here; and with the box. It's so good of you to have taken such good care of it.'

I mumbled something, I don't know what – I was incoherent.

She sat down alongside me and put her hands on the box.

'Syra, I'm so glad you have been looking after the box. I told you before about the master whose orders I lived for. Do you remember? He left me a list to carry out even after his death. Well, now I have only one instruction left – it is the very last from my master, Father Dawson...'

I looked up at her surprised. Suddenly I was filled with a new fear. The very mention of his name sent a surge of raw panic running through my veins. Father Dawson! Miranda's master!

'Ah, I see you are excited to hear his name. Yes, his final instruction compels me like no other. Shall I tell you what it is, Syra? Of course. "Miranda, my heart must remain with you all". That's what it said – nothing else – but I knew exactly what he meant. And now, thanks to you, Syra, I can fulfil my last obligation.'

She lifted the box from my knees. I couldn't stop myself from holding onto it, protecting it. She took each one of my hands one by one and removed them. My reactive resistance had passed, now I felt like a helpless puppet.

'Syra, you have done your duty now. You must let go. Now, at last, I have the organ which is both our heart and at our heart. This is the heart of our founder, the one who discovered the secret that lay within your blood, the one who brought you to us and gave us new life. And it is the heart of the one who sacrificed himself for us, giving his own life so that the flock should survive. And it is the heart which will be an endless supply of nourishment for the flock. It will remain forever the centre of their hopes and wishes. And Syra, you must return also. You must come with me back to the flock. They are waiting for the heart and for you. Can you imagine their joy, Syra?'

She shook her head dreamily, as if at last all her wishes had been granted.

I was dumbfounded. I didn't know what to think. I didn't know what to say.

I stared at her as she stood up. She turned to Anicka.

'Anicka, go and fetch the others. And make sure that the replacement for Sparky doesn't wander off. She's so absentminded.'

The sound of Sparky's name sent a shiver of anxiety and regret through me.

Anicka nodded, turned and set off on her mission. She was dressed exactly the same as when I had first seen her with Sparky outside Club Lichvář – pink tights, a black tight vest top and a spiky hemmed mesh skirt with glittering stars hanging from the spikes. Her hair was drawn up through a tightly pulled band into a vertical plume on top of her head; its bright red ends showered down like a storm of crimson rain. She bobbed across the concourse towards the female restrooms. Suddenly, without stopping, she leant to the side and swept up a briefcase momentarily untended by its owner. She hopped and skipped away, filled with excitement and, like a thieving jackdaw, clutching her latest prize in her long red talons.

Miranda turned back to me.

'These girls! But it's a good business, and the one that supports our work at Pacific Heights. Now that Pastor Wick is gone perhaps you might want to get more involved? His plan for you was a bad one anyway, Syra. How could he think of keeping you unconscious for the rest of your life? How do you see yourself as a slave trader?'

I couldn't answer.

She nodded to me to follow. I thought again of the flock, of Father Dawson. I wondered what my life would be like if I returned with Miranda – a source of nourishment for the flock, trafficking slaves, and goodness knows what else! My blood ran cold. I tried to clear my mind. I concentrated on two things: I knew the box was empty, and I knew I didn't intend to go with Miranda. They were the only two things I should think about – the only two things I should act on.

I jumped up and barged past Miranda.

'Here, you can keep the box!' I shouted as I ran as fast as I could across the concourse and out of the airport.

I jumped into a taxi and told the driver to go to Hlavné Námestie square. I thought we could work out something about the fare when we got there.

I sat back on the warm plastic seat. I breathed in deeply. I was free! Suddenly the world felt fresh. I listened to the driver's unintelligible conversation and watched him adjust his mirror so that he could see my bare knees. I opened them slightly and drew up the hem of my dress. I pulled my panties off and pulled up my dress so that my naked cunt was completely exposed. The pink slit at its centre glistened with moisture. I desperately wanted it filled. Yes, I desperately wanted a cock inside it, but not before I had felt the sting of punishment across my buttocks, the tightness of bonds around my ankles and wrists, and the confinement and lack of control that came with being completely under the instructions of another. A warm rush of anticipation and excitement flooded through me. I reached over the driver's seat and dropped my panties onto his lap. Yes, I'm sure we can work out something about the fare.

Turn the page for a taster of our next 3 titles

THE REINS OF POWER

by

Elizabeth Johns

PROLOGUE

With classic Chanel perfuming the air, the room was enveloped in darkness although outside the afternoon sun shone as bright and guileless as it had at midday when its occupants first arrived. The hastily drawn curtains had left a narrow slit through which the light struck the interior in a tall blade, like a laser beam in which the dust motes danced to the strains of passion, slicing straight through the concealing, comforting gloom and down to the rich carpet on which a pair of Kurt Geiger shoes lay discarded, the light revealing their colour as soft brown.

.In the twilight that suffused the rest of the room a woman and a man writhed energetically on the bed, instinctively reading each other's desires and alternately relinquishing or gaining the initiative as passion dictated, ever guiding each other onward toward the pinnacle. Accepting that her need was probably the greater, Natasha Fielding drew in ragged breaths to sustain her through the remainder of their time together.

Her dark hair was thrown chaotically across the pillows as their intertwined bodies stood out pale in their surroundings. His complexion was paler than her attractively desirable, golden tan which seemed to emphasise her sensual vitality.

With polished nails that had scarcely seen their natural state since Natasha's early teens, her long, elegant fingers sought purchase as they clawed at his sweat-beaded back. Lying beneath him with her long legs flung wide apart to allow him to penetrate her with welcoming ease, she hollowed her back and braced her feet to lift them both free of the bed in an effort to impale herself more gratifyingly on his wonderfully rigid shaft. After a couple of back-breaking seconds during which his lunges had speared her insides, she allowed him to take control once more and they dropped back on the bed. Then she wrapped her legs around his hips and, with widened eyes that took in his handsome features, she drew him closer to facilitate impossibly deep penetration.

Her cries were a strange mixture of passion and bridled respectability, "Oh! Oh God! Oh! Oh! God!" as his cock speared her belly deeply with blissfully agonising thrusts until her outpourings gave way to incoherent whimpers and wails as she thrashed her head from side to side on the pillows.

And then once more he assumed the leading influence rather than letting her have it all her own way. Withdrawing only slightly, gently but assertively he gripped her ankles and removed her legs from his hips and set her feet down on either side. Eliciting kitten-like mewls and gurgles of pleasure from her eminently kissable wide lips, he launched into a pattern that was more appropriate to his own needs. His pale, muscular buttocks and thighs worked between her magnificent spread thighs, rising and falling in a stabbing rhythm; a rhythm whose tempo increased until the room echoed with their ascending, abandoned cries of ecstasy. Her fluting ones were a tuneful descant above his guttural cries of triumphant release in their duet of carnality.

For a few moments their movements became frantic, then Justin froze, the veins in his neck standing rigid as ropes as his head was flung back at his climax and his thick seed began to seep out from between her glistening, still engorged nether lips.

And then they subsided into a tumbled embrace. Held against the hardness of his chest, Natasha drank in his sensuality and sighed, as if filtering rather than simply spilling the contents of her heart. Sex was one thing, she

SLAVES OF IRONTOWN

by

Adriana Arden

CHAPTER ONE

'Now take everything off,' Constable Colter told Melanie Paget briskly: 'clothes, boots, watch, jewellery, the lot.'

'We've got to have some full-length photos of you undressed for your criminal record,' Constable Mattock explained.

The three of them were standing in a small brightly lit room within Shackleswell Central police station. In front of Mel was a digital camera mounted on a tripod, while the wall behind her was marked with a big "X" of lines and circles like a target that incorporated a graduated height scale. The other furnishings comprised a metal locker, a small table on which rested a desktop printer, a couple of hard chairs and a large flat screen TV on a hinged frame folded back against one wall.

Mel was scared and miserable enough having just had her fingerprints taken without being confronted by this totally unexpected additional humiliation casually linked with the phrase: "criminal record." She gulped as fresh concern creased her pretty face, hoping she had misunderstood. 'You want to take pictures of me… naked?'

'That's way we process offenders like you in Shackleswell, girl,' said Colter, who was sandy-haired and of beefy build. 'Every physical detail gets recorded now so there's no chance of mistaken identity later. Those are the rules and you've got to obey them.'

'If you don't like it you shouldn't have done anything to get yourself arrested, should you?' Mattock, who was taller and darker, pointed out.

'But it was only for vagrancy,' Mel protested, thinking even as she spoke that it sounded such an old fashioned charge. 'I didn't know it was wrong. I was just looking round the town. I'm not a real criminal.'

'You were letting your own life go to waste,' Mattock said scathingly. 'That's criminal enough as far as we're concerned.'

'We take that sort of thing seriously in Shackleswell,' Colter added. 'This is a clean, efficient town. All waste gets collected up and properly recycled.'

'And it's all got to be recorded in the process,' said Mattock, tapping the camera meaningfully. 'Every detail.'

Mel felt sick and confused. Were they talking about picking litter off the street or people like her? Whatever it was it seemed they still expected her to strip-off, which she could not possibly do in front of two strange men even if they were in uniform. 'Can't you get a woman officer in to take the pictures?' she pleaded.

'There aren't any available,' said Mattock impatiently. 'Now hurry up. This isn't the time or place to come over all shy. You haven't got anything we haven't seen before. You're not the first foolish girl we've handled, you know, and you certainly won't be the last, so let's be having those clothes off.'

Mel chewed her lip nervously. They kept calling her "girl" as though she was a child when she was actually nineteen, and now they wanted to photograph her naked. This was not the way they did things in TV police series.

But then what did she know? After the terrible mistakes she had so recently made how could she trust her own judgement any more. Perhaps there were new procedures in place because of the threat of terrorism or differences between police forces. She felt the return of the brooding misery her arrest had briefly displaced. Did it matter? She had made her choices and this was where they had brought her. Any further shame she suffered was her fault. Perhaps after all she deserved it…

Taking a deep breath Mel shrugged off her anorak then stooped to untie her boots. As she handed over

FRUIT OF SUBMISSION
(A SEQUEL TO SEED OF SUBMISSION)

by

Robin Ballantyne

CHAPTER 1

'Cynthia?'

Silence. David Arundel sighed, and called his daughter again.

'Cynthia!' And, after another pause: 'The cab's here. Yves is waiting!'

'Coming!' There was the sound of hurried movement from upstairs. David turned to the tall young man at his side and shrugged. Yves shrugged back.

Moments later, Cynthia Arundel flew down the stairs, a full-length cape trailing after her. She was tall and slim, with pale skin and long hair of dark reddish-brown, and not for the first time David noticed how she looked very like her mother had, at that age. He smiled at his memories, and then kissed his daughter on the cheek.

'I hope you have a wonderful evening,' he said. 'Where are you going?'

She laughed. 'I haven't told Yves, and I won't tell you either. It's a surprise!'

Yves looked put out, and Cynthia took his hands. 'Please, darling! You did say I could go anywhere I liked, and you'll find out in a little while anyway.' She squeezed his hands then turned away. As she did so, David saw her expression change. Just for a second, he thought she looked almost calculating, but the look was gone as soon as he had noticed it. Then his daughter spun round, took Yves by one hand and pulled him towards the door.

'Come on,' she told her boyfriend. 'We'll be late!' As David watched, she dragged the bemused-looking Yves out of the house, and few moments later there was the sound of a car pulling away.

David listened as the sound faded. Then he shook his head, and closed the door. There was work to be done. Not unpleasant work, to be sure, but a duty all the same. He turned and walked back along the hall, up the sweeping flight of stairs that led to the upper floor of the handsome apartment, and into the drawing room where his wife was waiting for him.

At thirty eight years old, Julia Arundel was still a striking woman. Her waist, which would anyway have been trim, was pulled into a stern hourglass by the corset he made her wear. Together with the close-fitting red dress she wore over it, it emphasised the feminine curves which had been hers from adolescence, and which had been filled out delightfully by childbearing. Her auburn hair, not yet touched by grey, fell to the small of her back in a thick straight torrent.

Even after eighteen years of marriage, David found her deeply attractive. He allowed his gaze to roam over her for a moment, feeling himself stiffen at the sight of her. To his pleasure, she blushed slightly. Then her eyes fell to the collared girl who kneeled, naked, beside her. David followed her gaze, and smiled.

'Yolanda,' he said to the girl. 'You have not been good!'

She looked at the floor. David reached down and lifted her chin so that her eyes met his. 'In fact, you have been bad, haven't you?'

She nodded.

'You have become lazy and disobedient, haven't you?'

She nodded again, and a tear sprang from the corner of one eye.

'What happens to lazy disobedient girls?'

Her eyes slid away, and she whispered something. David tightened his grip on her chin. 'What did you say?'

He felt her stiffen for a moment. Then she repeated: 'They must be punished, Sir.'